THE ODDS

THE ODDS

A Novel

Jacqueline M. Ryan

iUniverse, Inc.
New York Lincoln Shanghai

The Odds

Copyright © 2007 by Jacqueline M. Ryan

All rights reserved. No part of this book may be used or reproduced by any means, graphic, electronic, or mechanical, including photocopying, recording, taping or by any information storage retrieval system without the written permission of the publisher except in the case of brief quotations embodied in critical articles and reviews.

iUniverse books may be ordered through booksellers or by contacting:

iUniverse
2021 Pine Lake Road, Suite 100
Lincoln, NE 68512
www.iuniverse.com
1-800-Authors (1-800-288-4677)

Because of the dynamic nature of the Internet, any Web addresses or links contained in this book may have changed since publication and may no longer be valid.

This is a work of fiction. All of the characters, names, incidents, organizations, and dialogue in this novel are either the products of the author's imagination or are used fictitiously.

ISBN: 978-0-595-46069-4 (pbk)
ISBN: 978-0-595-90367-2 (ebk)

Printed in the United States of America

For creative writing classes and their teachers.

CHAPTER 1

As I lit the bummed cigarette, I looked up at the New York City skyline, thinking what it would be like to live and work here. The sun was well behind the mammoth buildings with their lights slowly increasing, blending into the starlit night. The blending of dark buildings into the setting sun slowly ended as I watched the darkness engulf the city.

I sat on one of the numerous benches that lined Central Park South smoking a cigarette that was void of its usual magical powers. To me, a good cigarette always cleared the mind. Ten years ago when I was a non-smoker, I wouldn't have believed that, but age and worries have convinced me of its powers. Each drag on a butt made the night seem cooler, made the city lights brighter, made the mind clear. Except this time. This time the cigarette wasn't helping. This time, Payne, I thought, this time you'll have to make the decision yourself. Maybe the walk back to the hotel would help.

The Department of Alcohol, Tobacco and Firearms was transferring me to the New York office. I was getting a promotion by moving here from the Philadelphia office. It was a good offer. I knew I had to take it if I wanted to mover further up in law enforcement. It came with a lot of baggage. I would have to move from Philadelphia to New York. I would be traveling more, and I would have to decide what to do about my life in Philadelphia.

Part of that life was the current relationship I was in. It wasn't as if it was a really difficult decision. I knew it was time to move on personally and professionally. It was the conflict that would come with ending my two-year relationship that I wasn't looking forward to.

Taking the last drag on the cigarette, I glanced over my shoulder at Central Park. Central Park at night was something that had always fascinated me. Even as a young country kid, I was intrigued by it at night. Looking at the park, I put the cigarette out and stretched. I laughed aloud hearing a voice from my past, not sure if she was actually standing next to me.

She had laughed at me.

"I'm serious." I had said.

"Payne, I'm serious too." Her face took on that motherly look she often showed when I wanted to do something crazy. "I was born in this city, and I wouldn't walk through there at night."

I just looked down at her. For that moment she was like my mom and I tried what usually got me my way. I pouted. She wasn't giving in.

"If you want, I'll drive through it later." She said looking at me like I held the world for the asking. Like I was the world. I didn't know it, but I was the world to her. Even the city, her world, disappeared when she looked at me that night. And I destroyed that world.

I turned back to the noise on the street. I waited for a break in traffic and crossed Central Park South heading downtown on Fifth Avenue. New York always made me think of Chelsea, maybe because she introduced me to the city. Raised in central Pennsylvania, I had reached twenty before I had really been immersed in New York. She taught me what she called her rules for survival.

"This is what I tell all my green New Yorkers," she had said smiling at me. "Rule number one: don't look up. Rule number two: if someone asks you for money keep walking. Rule number three: if you can cross the street do it." Whenever I did something stupid she added rules on. The last time I saw her she had been on rule number fifteen. If I took the transfer, I'd have to look her up and let her continue. Eight years later.

I walked down Fifth Avenue watching the people rush in and out of buildings. It was the tail end of the rush hour. Rush hour; that was an out of date phrase. Some time, somehow that hour had turned into three. The evening commute in Manhattan was like nothing else in the world. The throngs of people moved in unison. They migrated downtown toward the hub of all activity, Grand Central Terminal. People watching was best done in New York and it was definitely at its best during the hours of commuting. The cabs raced by daring anyone to defy their right to be where they were going both individually and collectively. The sea of yellow cars set the pace of the rush hour traffic. They locked the cars and buses into their pace and motivated the people into moving faster and faster. I thought, if I took the transfer, I would become one of the many people moving with the swarm that was New York.

I don't know what caused me to turn and look. I realized the light had changed and the herd of people was moving again. I was crossing with the crowds and moving in time with the motion of the city when I saw her. Not her really just her picture. She was in the window of Barnes and Noble. The one on Fifty-seventh Street across from Carnegie Hall. They were doing a promotional. It seemed natural to me that she was in a bookstore. She always loved a bookstore while I loved a music store. We each brought that to each other. I began to tolerate bookstores and she began to experience music stores. It wasn't really her, but it felt like her. She was, if it could be possible, more mature. I had never been so affected by one person's picture. I was struck still. The masses of people moved around me; some irritated; others used to the oddity of their own, just moved around me. Over the initial shock of seeing Chelsea's picture in the window of Barnes and Noble, I moved forward to investigate.

"Holy Shit!" I said aloud as I opened the door and moved inside the warmth of the store. She had to be the most determined woman I had ever met. She once told me that she was going to have her picture hanging in the window of this particular Barnes and Noble. Although Barnes and Noble had expanded across the country with superstores, this was the one that she had first visited with her grandfather. This was the one that meant something to her. It was always an accomplishment she intended to make her own.

I walked over to the display that held her book. Initially, I couldn't believe she had done it. As I put more thought into it, I realized she was probably capable of anything. The things she accomplished before I entered her life astounded me. She was a remarkable woman then and even more so now. I picked up a copy. *The Hiding Place* by Chelsea Michaels. The book itself, at this moment, didn't interest me. I knew it was incredible. She always had a way with writing and I never did. I was more intrigued by the biography section on the jacket cover. I don't know what I hoped to learn about her that I didn't already know, but I read it the same. Born and raised in New York ... educated at Fairfield University ... Masters from Fordham University ... teaches at a private school for boys in New York City ... and I don't know why it was so important, but the one final missing statistic was the most important. There was no mention of a husband.

As I stood mesmerized over the book, a young sales clerk came up to me. He was tall, with blonde hair and glasses. Patrick was on his nametag. He was very young and very enthusiastic. He didn't ask me if I needed help, but rather just started talking to me.

"That's a fantastic book," he said in a deep voice. It seemed much too full for his age. I guessed he was around eighteen.

"Is it?" I asked politely. I flipped it over in my hand to look at the cover.

"Yeah. She comes in here all the time. You know that private school for boys? It's a few blocks over."

I looked up at him and thought, don't tell me this. Please don't tell me that she is here. But at the same time I was excited to hear of her. The day we said good-bye she told me, "Someday when you know where you're going and when I know where I'm going maybe we'll meet up again. Maybe...." I had the feeling that someday was here.

"What's the school's name?"

"Power Memorial? Ever hear of it? Kareem Abdul Jabbar graduated from there. It was closed for a while, but they reopened it recently. I'm actually a senior there this year."

"No kidding." I humored him and took the book to the counter. Let the kid think he sold me the thing. Anything to get him to stop talking. Next thing I would know he would be knocking off work to show me the way. I just wanted to pay for the damn book and continue on my way.

When I left the store, I felt the oddest sensation come over me. I had always been a man who had all the answers. I had to know what was going on and why. For the second time in my life, I didn't have the answers. For the second time, I didn't know why I was doing something. And again, it involved Chelsea. On impulse my hand went up. I stood on the curb waiting for a cab, any cab. I don't know how long I waited for one to finally stop. It was six thirty and the rush was still on. I was determined to see Chelsea. I stepped into the cab, hoping I wasn't making another mistake.

"Where to?" he asked methodically turning the meter on.

"Power Memorial High School. Know where it is?" I asked looking at the badge tacked to the dashboard. Jesus Rodriguez.

"Up by Lincoln Center." He pulled out into traffic thrusting the cab headlong into the sea of midtown traffic. Jesus had the pre-game show on. The Yankees were playing that night in one of the first games of the postseason. I listened while I watched the traffic alongside of us. He had the most erratic driving. He moved into the left hand lane cutting off a bus that was, I feel, as determined as Jesus to get where he wanted to go. Except for the fact that the bus outweighed and over powered the tin yellow box I was in, I would have been appreciative of the man's courage. It was when he cut across the street totally to the right and made the sharp turn onto Fifty-third Street, I regretted my decision to pursue this madness inside me; yet I couldn't stop it if I wanted to. There was nothing I could do but wait out the ride. I was out of control; Jesus was out of control.

"What do you want to do?" She had asked me. "Where do you want to go?"

It was my first trip to the city. She took me to a toy store. Perhaps the largest one I'd ever seen; FAO Schwartz.

"Come on." She pulled my hand, "We'll take a cab. You have to experience that. You are without a doubt too green to go on the subway. But a cab ride, you might enjoy. It's an entire subculture of the city."

That's what she told me. I was never so frightened as when I stepped out of that first cab ride. She had just laughed and said, "Worse than driving with me?" I smiled as I remembered that and thought but not worse than driving with Jesus. This was perhaps the wildest drive I had ever been on. Even the drunken rides home from house parties or bars were better.

"Any particular place, or just Lincoln Center?" Jesus asked.

"This is fine." At this point I just wanted out. I handed him the money and jumped out like the seat of the cab was on fire. I walked over to the hot dog stand. I remembered these guys as being friendly as long as you bought something off them.

"Can of Coke?" I asked taking out my wallet. "Which way is Power Memorial High School?"

"Two blocks south and its right across from Fordham University by St. Paul the Apostle."

"Thanks," I said handing him the money.

I set out with my can of Coke and my nagging conscience. What if she didn't want to see me? I couldn't blame her. I wouldn't want to see me. What if she wasn't there? It was almost seven. Any other moron would be home. Somehow I knew she would be there. If she hadn't changed, she would be working late. She always worked late. Before I knew it, the school was there. There were a couple of lights still on. Probably only maintenance men.

I walked into the old building, wandering the halls. Finally I found a whistling janitor. He was old and jovial. Yes, Miss Michaels was still there. She was in her classroom, one-twelve. Her classroom. It sounded strange to hear. She had always joked in college saying, "I'm going to be in school for the rest of my life, but this time I'm sitting at the BIG desk."

When I arrived at her room, I stood at the door, watching her through the window in the door. She was sitting at her desk. Her papers were spread around her. She had taken her suit jacket off and put in on the back of her chair. The hunter green skirt that came to just below her knees was a classic look with her white silk blouse. She was leaning over a stack of papers with her hair swept off her face the way she did in college. She took a pencil and wrapped her hair around it creating a bun that the pencil could slip through. It was a fascinating procedure to watch. I watched her do it one night just after I met her. She was bent over an

English paper obviously frustrated with it and then her hair that kept streaming into her face. I watched as she took her long auburn hair in her hand and created this improvisation.

I smiled amazed that she still kept this practice. Almost ten years later, and she was still using the pencil trick as she called it. She was so unaware of her womanhood; so unaware of her appeal; both then and now. I was content to watch. Content to see the woman that the girl I met in college had grown into. Like many redheads, how she hated that phrase, she had such fair skin with freckles. She had always been told she was the spitting image of her mother. I could see her mother now in the woman she had become.

As I watched, she kicked off her shoes and pulled her legs up underneath her and in that second I saw the top of her gartered stocking. That made the smile reach my eyes. She always wore stockings. She was the first woman I had met that almost always wore a garter belt. Once I asked her why she wore them. She had smiled at me pushing her hair from one side to the other and said, "Have you ever worn pantyhose?"

"No." I answered smiling back at her and she explained it in one easy analogy: like being a sausage in its casing.

As I watched, I realized she was getting tired. School had been out for almost four hours and still she was grading papers. Her left hand rose to her earlobe. She began tugging on it like she always did when she was tired. She told me once she had been doing it since she knew where her ear was and that her family had tried to break her of the habit for what seemed centuries. Nothing had worked. They couldn't break her of it, and that made me happy. It was the little girl inside her; the girl who would fight with me and wrestle the remote control away from me.

I opened the door and walked in.

CHAPTER 2

I was sitting at my desk trying to get the last few essays graded. It was almost seven on a Thursday night. I should have been home getting ready to watch the Yankees in the first round of the play offs. The door to my classroom opened. Jimmy, the head custodian always stopped by between six-thirty and seven to remind me that it was getting late and I should head home.

"I swear Jimmy, I'm leaving after this one." I said without looking up.

"So you finally made it to the big desk," said a voice I hadn't heard in eight years.

I looked up at the door in amazement. There stood a ghost to me; a ghost that had left my life eight years ago to find his life. He was standing at my door in a classic navy business suit, arms across his chest, his brown hair, as always, slightly out of place. He was as sure of himself as he was ten years ago when I met him. I couldn't believe he was standing there. I finally got up from my desk.

I was suddenly very aware of my appearance. I thought what a mess I must be. I took the pencil out of the hasty bun I had put my hair up while I was grading papers. "Look what the cat dragged in."

"It's just me," he said walking toward my desk.

I was so taken off guard by him, I didn't know what to do. I walked toward him and realized I had no idea what to say or do. It had been so long. When Payne and I had broken up years ago, it was a very difficult time for me. I was still so very much in love with him. In fact, it had taken me years to forgive him and trust someone again. He had made it clear he didn't want to be in a relationship with me then and I wasn't really sure what it meant to have him show up at my door now.

There was a silence between us that could only be measured in years. All the years had gone by and neither one of us knew what to say. How does one greet a lover after numerous years? It was a first for both of us. Finally I broke the silence, heavy with a thousand questions.

"Give me a hug, you pain in the ass." I said as I opened my arms to give him a hug. I embraced him and held him close revealing in the feel of having his arms around me again. We separated and he stared down at me.

"So this is your room. You made it to the big time," he joked looking around. "Christ, its bigger than my office."

"And everyone pitied me when I told them I was going into teaching." I stood there hands on my hips looking intently at him. "What's new and exciting?"

To my surprise, he pulled out my book from inside his raincoat. "I was hoping for a personal reading or at least a book signing." He walked over to my desk. "I see you're working late, as usual."

I laughed nervously. My desk hadn't changed since college. It was a hopeless mass of papers. He had told me once he wondered how I found anything in college when it was just my papers. Now with all my students' papers it was all the more crazy, but I knew where everything was. Organized chaos. He picked up an essay.

The River Valley Civilizations. "How many more do you have to grade?" he asked.

"Five more. I think. I'm behind in grading them. I've been doing book stuff on the weekends. A different city every weekend. It's been rough, not that I'm complaining," I said with a smile.

"Could I tear you away for a late dinner?" He asked as he put the essay down and leaned against the desk. I was very hesitant about the offer. "My treat. You paid last time we went out."

"Yeah. That's right I did. I'm game. Where do you want to go?" I asked as I walked past him putting on my shoes and my suit jacket.

"Some place close by where we can sit down and talk. How about the place we went the night of the opera?" he asked

"The Gingerman," I said packing up the last few essay papers in my briefcase. "Just let me get my coat and we're set."

I walked over to the closet, grabbed my raincoat, and put it on. I pulled my hair out from under the collar and walked over to the desk. "Where did I put my keys? I'm always losing them. I'd lose my head if it wasn't attached."

Payne laughed. "You haven't changed much have you Chels." In college, I lost my keys at least once a day. I was so nervous with him standing there that it seemed a desperate search.

I rummaged through my top draw and said, "Shut up before I hit you." I continued to search fruitlessly and then stopped to think. I put my hand in my suit jacket pocket and pulled out my keys. I held them up smiling at him. We laughed together.

I turned the lights off and locked the door taking my briefcase with me. We walked down the hall until we reached another classroom with lights on. Jimmy, the head custodian was inside. He was busy washing a blackboard.

"Jimmy," I said softly, "I'm leaving, I locked up my classroom."

"Did that man find you?" He asked. Payne was behind me in the hallway.

"Yes." I answered.

"Nice looking guy. Your boyfriend?" I began to clutch tighter at my briefcase handle as I looked back at his smiling face.

"Not exactly." I said.

"Well he should be," he said continuing to wash the board. Payne laughed and I smacked him. Thanks a lot Jimmy, I thought. Payne needed a boost to his ego like New York City needed more cars.

"I'll see you tomorrow," I said to Jimmy and briskly began to walk down the hall. Not surprisingly, Payne kept pace with me easily. I'm about five feet eight inches tall while Payne is just over six feet tall. I was angry about what Jimmy had said. I felt embarrassed that he had said that in front of Payne. Whenever I am angry, I always walk faster. This situation was no different.

"Is this the New York City Marathon?" He asked. I slowed the pace and looked at him. I smiled and shook my head.

"Sorry, I just remembered how hungry I was." I lied. What made it more difficult was the look he gave me. He knew I was lying. I always said I could never lie. Lies were written all over my face. This time was no exception. He knew I was angry that Jimmy had said that in front of him, but I wasn't going to admit it. I could never stand the way he gloated when he was right. For some reason, he let it slide.

We stepped out onto the street and headed uptown toward Lincoln Center. The traffic had died down to a slight herd of cabs and cars every now and then. Crossing the side streets was no longer difficult, but all the same I couldn't wait to goad him about my rules. I said, "I can see you remember rule number three. Cross the street when you can."

He laughed at my predictability.

"What are you doing in town?" I asked.

"Meeting with superiors. I'm with ATF now."

"You work in town?" I asked surprised. I still thought of him as the country kid that he was that first year in college.

"Not yet, but I may be." I raised my left eyebrow at him. It was an interesting sign of inquiry; one that many people could do. Payne, however, couldn't and he always loved when I did it.

As we walked past Lincoln Center, he asked if I had been to the opera lately.

"Not lately, but one of priests that teaches at the school wanted to take a class trip there. I told him I recommended *Faust*. Especially for total fools who had never been to the opera before."

"Now we're gonna fight," he said pushing me slightly. *Faust* was the opera I took him to for one of our first dates. He had never been to the opera and was completely lost. I bought him a libretto and introduced him to a type of music he never knew existed.

"Someone had to give you some culture," I remarked smartly. We crossed Broadway and walked up West Sixty-fifth Street to the restaurant.

To Payne, New York City was always a confusing place. To me, it was an easy place to find your way around in. In reality, it was easy to find your way around most of Manhattan. As I explain to most of my high school students, midtown Manhattan is laid out in a grid. I had lived in Queens most of my life and I had traveled in and out of Manhattan regularly. I always knew where I was, even when I didn't know where I was going. One day I was a few blocks off when Payne noticed. I told him, "We're not lost. We're exploring."

We walked into the Gingerman and sat at a table in the small glass enclosed porch. It was just as I remembered it. I hadn't come back to the restaurant since that date. We were here ten years ago, both young, both nervous about being out to dinner with each other. I looked at him over my menu and I knew he had the same thought. We both laughed.

"I can't believed the waiter thought we were married," I said laughing. "We were so young. I felt like saying, 'Sure my four kids are home with the baby-sitter.'"

"You should have. Besides, we weren't that young."

"Compared to the old couple next to us we were." I said and continued to laugh and he just watched smiling. He had told me once that he loved to see me smile and laugh.

The waiter came and took our order. After we were settled with our drinks, he began grilling me about my life and I pried into his. We both knew things about each other and the paths we took. He knew I had graduated from Fairfield when we both should have. He knew that from the mutual friends we had. He left Fairfield University after an academically disastrous sophomore year. It was part of the demise of our relationship. He had a problem with the distance. He also had a problem with the intensity of a relationship with me. He had partied a little too much and hadn't taken school as serious as he should have. After two years of college, he had transferred all the courses that could be transferred to St. Francis University in Pennsylvania. He had lost a year and finished school the year after I finished at Fairfield University.

"How did you end up working at Power Memorial?" he asked.

"I applied right out of Fairfield. It was a great location; right next to Fordham. I could get my masters very easily. I just walked to class after teaching all day."

"That's got to be a long commute every day from Long Island." He stated. My parents had moved while I was in college from Queens further out east on Long Island.

"Not really. I never really liked the new house in Hicksville. I think it was the name of the town. When I took the job at Power

Memorial and enrolled in graduate school, I moved in with my grandfather in Astoria."

"How is he?" he asked.

"He died about three years ago," I said simply, looking down at my drink. My grandfather had been around the house a few times when Payne was in town. He had retired from the NYPD when I was born but hadn't really lost the tough guy attitude in the twenty-five years he had been retired.

"I'm sorry," he said genuinely. He knew I had always been close to my grandfather. I was named after the section of the city that he patrolled as a beat cop.

"He had cancer and really didn't want to live that much longer without his wife. So now the house is mine. It felt weird moving into the upstairs. I was living in the basement apartment while he was alive. That way I had my space and he had his. After he passed away, I moved upstairs and a few people have come and gone in the basement apartment. Right now my cousin Susan is living upstairs with me."

Our dinner arrived and we began eating. I then asked about his life.

"How did you end up working for ATF?" I asked.

"After I graduated from Saint Francis University with my degree in Criminal Justice, I completed my masters at St. Joseph's University in Philadelphia. That included an internship with ATF. After I graduated I applied to work in the field office. Surprisingly I was offered the job. Now they want to move me to New York." he said with a smile. "That's why I'm in town; actually on my way out of town. I'm due back in Philly tomorrow night.

I glanced at my watch. It was after nine. I was beginning to get really tired. I had three glasses of wine and I still had a long subway ride home. I motioned for the check. When it arrived, Payne paid, as promised. I grabbed my briefcase and we shuffled out the door. I didn't want him to go back to his lonely hotel room. Rather I wanted to spend more time with him. I wanted to know if there was something still there, but I didn't want to be the one who made the first move. One of the things I always regretted was being the one to make the first move. As we stepped outside, he said something that shocked me and seemed like a first move to me.

"I'd love to see your house." He said.

"Tonight?" I asked. My eyebrow was up again.

"If you don't mind." I had never wanted to say no so badly. I wanted to take him home with me, but I knew it was complicated. I wanted this night with him almost as badly as the last night we spent together. I remembered my parting words to him.

"*You broke my heart, but I still love you. I think I'll always love you,*" I was crying.

"*Life right now is too complicated for us to go on seeing each other once a month.*" He had said, "*I need to finish school; get my life together. I've already messed up once. I can't mess up again.*"

I knew that he meant messing up in school, but it felt like he was messing up again. He had been messing up with me. I guess I was too much of a distraction and too much of an investment at the time. Somehow, I felt like tonight was the opportunity to give him a second chance.

"No. I don't mind," I said. "I don't mind at all. In fact, I've always wanted you to see the house. I think you'd like it."

"So lead the way. Cab or Subway?"

"Let's take the subway. You don't still stumble when it starts?" I asked. One of the first subway rides I took him on, he wasn't ready for the force of the subway pulling out of the station. We had been standing and he almost fell to his knees. I had threatened him that I would step over his body and leave him there because I was mortified to be seen with such an obvious green New Yorker.

"Very funny. I only did that once. But you know I have no idea how to get to the correct line or even remotely the right line to take."

"No problem." I said as I began to lead the way. We walked the few blocks to the N line and headed down the steps.

"Your going to have to get one of these if you plan to move to this town." I pulled out two Metrocards at the turnstile. "I always carry an extra one. Aren't you lucky."

Once inside the subway car, he began to ask me about *The Hiding Place*. He wanted to know what it was about. I was a little frightened that he now had a copy of it. I thought that he might recognize some of himself in the main character. I had created this cop that had his personality; his looks; his edge.

"I started writing it in college. Right after you left. I would put it down. I would pick it up. Then there was the search for an agent and a publisher. All of that finally came together around six months ago." I took a breath and moved my hair from one side to another, a nervous habit I'd had since I was a child. "It's a cop thriller. I started it with my grandfather's help and its kind of bittersweet now that it is in print and he's not around."

"So what has it been like promoting it?"

I laughed, "Crazy. It took up most of my summer and now it's eating into my fall. Every weekend is a new city. The only plus is all the frequent flier miles I am building up. I'm hoping to get someplace fun sometime this summer."

"Is Philly on your list anytime soon?"

"Actually, I think in about two weeks I have to make a trip down there," I said with a smile. "We're the next stop."

At Ditmars Boulevard, we left the subway and headed down the street. Before we knew it we were at the three-story row house.

"Wow. It's beautiful," he said.

CHAPTER 3

The row house was brick with wide front windows, a wooden door with a small keyhole stained-glass window, and a small stained-glass window directly above the door. There was stone walkway off the sidewalk that wound through a small grass lawn that was enclosed with waist high evergreen shrubs. It led to a brick and stone font porch that was about six steps up and included a brick and stone porch. The porch had a retractable green and white awning. The concrete driveway was to the right of the two connected houses and was shared with the left house of the pair next door. The entrance to the small downstairs apartment was off the driveway.

She began the walk up the stone walkway. I was left awestruck by the simple beauty of the house along the beauty of the woman who now owned the house. She stopped at the top of the staircase. Smiled and waved me on. I took the stairs quickly. I couldn't wait to see the inside of the house.

The front vestibule had a small closet to the left behind the opened front door and a glass inner door before you entered the front hallway. To the left were the stairs to the upstairs. They were mahogany hardwood with a burgundy oriental runner. The front hall had the same hardwood floor with a matching runner for the hallway. From the front hall a light could be seen in the kitchen through the glass paned door.

I walked into the front hall after her. She put her briefcase down by the stairs and began to take off her raincoat. After she had hers off and hung up she motioned for me to take my coat off. I took off my raincoat and suit jacket revealing my gun. She hung up the coat and then took out lock box from the top of the closet.

"Do you want to stash your gun in here? I actually keep my grandfather's gun in here."

"Sounds like a good idea." I said taking the gun and holster off as she took a key from the back of the door. She unlocked the strong box and I put the gun inside with her grandfather's old service revolver. She re-locked it and put it back in the top of the closet and hung up the key on the back of the door.

"Come into the living room," she said as she walked past me through the large open archway that led into the living room on the right.

It wasn't a large living room by any standards but it was beautiful. It had the original molding from the 1940s on the ceiling. They had been stained dark to match the mahogany floor. In the center of the hardwood floor was a room sized Oriental rug that matched the runners on the steps and in the hallway. She had a sage green couch along one wall and two matching chairs placed in front of the large front windows. Along the wall that separated the hallway from the living room was a piano. Above the piano was a collection of family pictures. I recognized some of her family. Her brother, her cousins, her mom and dad's wedding picture, her grandfather in his police uniform, her father in his naval uniform all in a variety of frames above the piano. More were on top of the piano. There was a small entertainment center in the right corner of the living room that held all the necessary electronic equipment to qualify as a media center.

Through a matching archway was the dining room. It had a small crystal chandelier over a small table. The china cabinet was against the right wall while the sideboard was against the left. Against the back wall were two built in bookshelves. A pair of windows separated the two bookshelves and overlooked a small raised stone patio. In the far left corner was a door leading into what I correctly guessed was the kitchen.

"I haven't really done much to the dinning room as of yet. I started with the living room a couple of years ago. I had a painter strip the white off the molding and restore the wood finish as well as paint the walls. I purchased a new living room set from Pottery Barn but kept the original tables and the piano. I, however, have no idea who any of those people are above the piano."

I laughed at her obvious joke. She walked through the dining room and into the kitchen. I followed her a little lost and very intrigued.

The kitchen was very much what a 1950s kitchen would look like. The floor was black and white tiled floor with a small table with a wrap around booth and a few diner style chairs. While the appliances were new, they fit in with the décor. The cabinets had glass panes in them and were painted pristine white. There was a door leading into a small bathroom and then out onto the porch.

"Do you want a drink?" she asked and I nodded in response.

"Do you still like Carlsberg?" she asked as she opened the refrigerator door.

"Sure. You haven't done much in here yet either."

"It's kind of hard to redo a kitchen. I was going to do it this past summer, but I redid the bathroom upstairs instead. That was a major project that ate up most of my book advance and my patience for doing renovation work while living here. I was able to do the bathroom this summer because I was almost never here and Susan temporarily moved into the basement after the last renter left."

"How is Susan?" I asked. Her cousin Susan was a very blunt person and loved to tell people where to go, what to do and how to get there. She was six months older than Chelsea and took her role as the elder very seriously.

"She just finisher her MBA at NYU. She has a job working for Time Warner right now. She may make a move sometime soon if something opens up. She actually just got engaged this summer and is planning a big wedding for the spring. She and her fiancé are at the Yankees game tonight."

"And what's your brother up to these days?"

"He's a Captain with the fire department now. He's married to Julie and they have two really cute kids. They bought a house out in Brooklyn in a really great neighborhood."

"That's great. I'll admit I was a bit concerned about him after September Eleventh. I'll admit I even checked the lists on line to make sure he was OK."

"We were lucky that day. No one in our immediate family was hurt. A few guys in Tommy's firehouse didn't make it. It was tough. He worked at Ground Zero daily trying to help out."

We had been drinking Carlsberg the whole time. I had finished my bottle and put it in the sink. I remembered she liked to rinse the bottles before recycling them while I just threw them back in the box and let the debris and backwash grow into something short of penicillin.

I stood in front of the sink and looked out into the backyard. It had a small green lawn and two one-car garages standing next to each other. There was a white picket fence separating her neighbor's backyard from hers and a cute patio set on the back porch.

I turned back around to see her staring at me. I smiled and leaned against the sink. "What about the rest of the house? You said there was a basement apartment. Let's check that out. I'll need a place to live if you're up for renting it."

She laughed, "You and I living under the same roof. That's a dangerous thing. Come on I'll show it to you and you can decide."

We went to a door off the main hallway that fell underneath the staircase. She opened it and there was a small pantry with a set of stairs leading to the basement. She pulled on the light, an old-fashioned light bulb with a string attached to it. As she led the way, I couldn't help looking at her ass. She always had the smallest butt I had ever seen.

I was smiling in my own little world when we reached the bottom of the stairs and she opened a door into the apartment. It was a pretty average sized living room with a small eating area off the kitchen. The kitchen was for the most part a row of appliances. As we traveled down the narrow hallway that led to the back bedroom she was telling me about the apartment.

"My brother Tommy's buddy Steve lived here while he did his residency in the city. It was perfect for him. He didn't want to spend a load of money on an apartment that he would most likely never be in. His parents had sold their house in Bellerose and moved to the Hamptons. That was too far to commute to work eighteen-hour days at the hospital. He bought a practice in the Boston area in June and moved up there."

The back bedroom was large enough to have a queen-size bed and dresser in it. I thought to myself that I could be really comfortable here. The bathroom was small with only a shower stall but it would suffice.

"What do you charge for rent?" I asked.

"I don't think you want this apartment Payne. I know the landlady, she's a real bitch." She laughed and pulled my hand to the staircase. "Come on I'll show you what ate up my advance."

"What exactly did you do to the bathroom upstairs?" I asked and we began the climb back up the stairs. I was all the more pleased to follow her up the stairs due to the fact that her cute little ass was now about two inches from my face. I couldn't see the outline of any panties and began to remember her extensive lingerie collection. At one point in college I actually had her count her bras. The number reached well into the fifties. Before I knew it, we were climbing the second set of stairs to the upstairs.

At the top of the stairs was a small hallway. There were four doors off the hallway with an obvious hall closet.

"The first door is an office. It used to be a very small bedroom. My dad's at one point," she said as she opened the door. The walls were painted a very subtle yellow with blue and yellow curtains. Inside were two desks. Each was in an opposite corner. Each had an overstuffed chair and rows of books lined the wall. Each desk had its own computer on top of it.

Chelsea motioned to the other door, "That's Susan's room and I don't dare open the door for fear of its state."

The last two doors were obviously the master bedroom and the bathroom. She opened the bathroom door and I was blown away. There was a platform Jacuzzi tub tucked into the far left corner under the stain-glassed window I had admired from outside. Next to the tub was a partition wall revealing an old-fashioned style toilet. In the corner behind the door was a stained-glassed shower stall large enough for two people. An old fashioned sink was in the center of the right wall between the shower stall and the toilet. Along the left wall there were towel racks and a door leading into the master bedroom.

"There was only the one door into the bathroom originally. There was a tub where the sink is now and the sink was where the tub now sits. The shower stall had walls around it instead of the stained glass. And the whole thing was a peach tile." She explained as she opened the door into her bedroom.

I followed her into the master bedroom. There was a queen size bed with an ornate headboard. There were two matching dressers and a vanity table.

"Is this the original bedroom set?" I asked as I walked around the room touching the furniture.

"Sort of." She said with a smile. "The bed was only a full-sized bed. I tried for about a year or so to sleep in it but it wasn't quite big enough. So I bought a queen sized mattress and took the head and footboard to a designer and asked him to keep the original design in mind but to make it large enough for a queen-sized bed."

I looked at it close up. "He did a great job." I had made a hobby out of making furniture and appreciated craftsmanship.

She stood at the vanity table watching me carefully. She seemed nervous to me. She walked over to the windows that overlooked the street. I walked over to her and stood behind her.

"Payne," she began, "I'm not sure what's going on with you right now. I'm a little too busy right now with work and the book to really think about the complications of tonight."

I was a little stunned. This was new for her. She had never really voiced the obvious. I guess she had changed a little. I went to stand behind her. She turned around and looked me in the eyes. There was confusion and sadness in her deep blue eyes, but there was also love.

I hugged her to me. I had missed the way she fit in my arms. Her head came up to my shoulders and it rested nicely there. She looked up at me and I bent my head and kissed her. I was hesitant; she was hesitant. But the sparks were still there.

Before I knew it, I was desperately unbuttoning the white silk blouse. There was an urgency to the first time we had been together in eight years. She unzipped the back of her skirt and stepped out of it. I was awestruck. She was still as beautiful as I remembered. She was in better shape than she had been in college, if that was possible. She had rowed for Fairfield and had an unbelievable body then, but now it was astonishing.

I had missed her underwear. It was always something out of a lingerie catalog. Her bra and panties always matched. It was a compulsion of hers. Her collection of lingerie included a variety of different under-garments. In college I had been more experienced in bed, but she clearly knew her way around a lingerie store. She explained the difference between camisoles and teddies and everything in between. She had a collection of camisoles that probably took up an entire side of a walk-in closet. Beyond being the first woman I knew to actually regularly use a garter belt, she had been the first woman I knew to wear a thong. While everyone wears them now, when we were in college it was a rarity. She was always ahead of the crowd.

We had moved slowly over to the bed and before I knew it, she was pulling me down to the bed with her by my tie. Next thing I knew she said, "I think you should know I'm not much into casual sex."

"I'm still wearing a tie, how can it be casual." She laughed and smiled.

"Let's fix that then." She pulled the tie off and we fell to the bed.

CHAPTER 4

I was laughing at his comment about the tie when we landed on my bed. We were laughing as we fell down on the bed, but it quickly became very heated and serious. I was wearing my bra, underwear, and stockings. Payne was still wearing his open shirt without the tie and his pants. I began pulling at his shirt urgently. He was kissing my neck and grabbed my earlobe in his mouth with his teeth. My ears were always very sensitive spots. The old-fashioned blowing in your ear actually did do something for me. He obviously remembered that. As I was pulling at his shirt, he was quickly removing my stockings. It always amazed me that he could multi-task while we were rolling around in bed. Once he would start to suck on my earlobe I could barely concentrate on one thing. Yet before I knew it he had unclipped both of the garters and was pushing down the stockings.

I had finally gotten his shirt off and was faced with his undershirt. He must have realized that would be impossible to remove while continuing to kiss me and moved away long enough for him to pull it over his head quickly. As he did that, I quickly reached behind my back and unhooked my bra. I took the bra off and tossed it off the side of the bed. He had quite frankly joked one night out with friends that he was definitely a boob man. One of his friends then laughed and said, "With Chelsea's rack you had better be, or I'd have to deck you."

"My god I missed your breasts." He said immediately bending his head to kiss them. He took his time caressing them slowly. I just closed my eyes and arched up into his hands. While it may have been a joke that he was a boob man, I was never really that much into my breasts. They were always too large for me. I spent most of my teenage years trying to cover them up with large sweaters and sweatshirts. I hadn't worn a bikini until I was a senior in high school because of the attention it drew to my breasts. My other boyfriends had never been as skilled in caressing my breasts and at times they were an annoyance. Not with Payne. So I was rather thankful that he was a boob man. He could evoke feelings that I never imagined could come from my breasts.

On this night he was spending his time with "the girls" as he had always called them. He was caressing the sides slowly before moving on to my nipples. By this point I was writhing in the unbelievable pleasure that only Payne had ever been able to give me. He took my right nipple into his mouth and began to gently caress it with his tongue. At about this point, I began to moan. It was a soft moan that took him by surprise. He paused and asked, "You always loved that. Do you want more?"

"Yes." I gasped as I began to pull at his belt.

He moved to my left breast and began to skillfully stroke at it with his tongue. While he was sucking on my left nipple, he was stroking my right breast. Soon he was tugging at my right nipple while he gently sucked at the left one. I was pulling at his belt panting. He had moved up onto his knees giving me access to his belt buckle, zipper and the waistband of his pants. I don't know how I managed to get his belt unbuckled and his pants unbuttoned and unzipped but I did. I was in such a state of arousal that I was beyond recollection. Before I knew it I was headed toward a climax that I hadn't had in years and he had only been caressing my breasts.

"Let go baby. It's ok." I heard him say against my left breast. It was as if I needed the words from him. He went back to caressing my right nipple with his tongue with his left hand making its way down to my panties. He quickly had his hand inside my underwear and had inserted his finger inside me as I screamed in pleasure at the waves of the orgasm rolled over me. My legs began to shake.

"Babe?" He said against my mouth. I kissed him passionately. He broke away and whispered in my ear, "Do you have any condoms?"

I scooted over to the edge of the bed and opened the nightstand. I was stretched out reaching into drawer. He took advantage of the pause to remove his boxers and began kissing my body again. Since I scooted across the bed, his head was no longer at my neck and breasts but lower. He began moving down my stomach toward my pubic area. Before I knew it he was kissing my inner thighs as I was trying to rummage through the top drawer by feeling for a condom wrapper.

His hands gently spread my legs as he began to move further up my legs. As his tongue touched me intimately, I finally grasped what I had been searching for and moaned loudly again bringing my hand down to his head. He was quickly sending me into another fevered pitch with his mouth when I grabbed his hand and pressed the wrapped condom into it.

"Payne." I moaned as he paused long enough to unroll the condom on his penis. The first time I tried to put a condom on him, he had been so excited by the touch of my hands on him that he immediately had an orgasm. From that moment on, whenever we used a condom, I was never allowed to do it.

He finally lay on top of me with his penis waiting to enter my body. I could feel him there and wanted him inside me so badly. I tried to move up against him to force him inside me, but he refused to allow that to happen. He smiled down at me and began to push inside me. I arched up to take more of him inside me and he pulled back. He was teasing me.

"Tell me what you want." He said staring down into my eyes. He was leaning on his elbows looking into my eyes. He had taken my hands in his hands and had them pinned up by my head. He probed a little deeper and withdrew.

"You." I gasped as I arched up again. He bent down and kissed my mouth sweetly licking my lips until I opened my mouth and sucked his tongue into my mouth. He moved inside me again and I whispered, "Please Payne."

He pushed inside me with his full body weight. There was fullness that had always been there when Payne was embedded in me completely. I gasped against his lips and he let go of my hands. I reached behind him and grabbed his ass. He had begun moving slowly at first. He would push inside me hard and fast and then slowly withdraw from me almost completely and sink back inside again. My hands grabbed at him anywhere I could get at him. I'm sure I made many marks up and down his back. I was so out of control, I began to move against him quickly. He began to speed up the thrusts until he was out of control. He grabbed my ass in his hand and thrust into me so deeply the headboard was banging loudly against the wall with thunderous booms. I was thankful that my bed was up against an outside wall and that no one was home to hear my screams of pleasure and the loud banging of the bed. I was panting so heavily my mouth was dry. Finally he thrust three final times and with a scream my whole body began to shake as his finally came into me one last time with wave after wave of pulsing.

He collapsed on top of me with a groan. He was panting and his heart was beating so fast I could feel it against my chest. I was gently stroking his back and neck playing with the back of his hair. He began to kiss my neck and leaned up to look at me. I had tears running down my face. I had begun to cry with the release of the final orgasm he gave me. He kissed the tears and said quietly, "Shh. Please don't cry."

He began to move out of me and I arched up to keep him inside me. I closed my eyes and sucked in my breath. "Not yet." I said. "I love having you inside me."

He was content to stay there for a few minutes but I knew it wouldn't last. He moved again and slid out of my body as I groaned. He kissed me quickly getting out of bed and into the bathroom to remove the used condom. When he came back, I had pulled up the sheets over my naked body. While I had a large collection of negligees to wear to bed, I had learned to sleep in the nude after sex. Payne had taught me to enjoy that like so many other things. One of our first nights sleeping together he said bluntly, "Why bother getting dressed when odds are I'll want to make love to you again before we get out of bed." There was something decadent about lying in bed naked with him.

Payne lay in bed with me drifting closer and closer to sleep. His deep green eyes were slowly closing for longer and longer periods of time. I had my head resting up on my elbow and was stroking his chestnut brown hair back from his forehead. His eyes were slowly closing and I kissed him sweetly on the lips. He smiled and said, "I missed you."

"I missed you too." I responded. His eyes finally closed and his breathing became even and deep. I had always admired that. He had the ability to fall asleep at a moments notice while I had battled insomnia all my life. In college, He would often fall asleep hard and fast while it would take me about a half an hour to an hour to wind down from any activity but especially from sex.

I rolled over and set the alarm. I wasn't looking forward to the alarm the following morning. I had an early morning meeting at school that was going to be difficult to make on a good morning. My lifestyle had changed in the years since college. I was no longer able to go for hours on little to no sleep. I needed my sleep. I needed more than five hours sleep. It was after midnight and it would be a short but memorable sleep in bed with Payne.

The alarm sounded too early the next morning. While I normally will snooze at least once, I immediately got out of bed. I grabbed my robe and headed into the bathroom. I was turning on the water in the shower when Susan walked into the bathroom.

"Chelsea, what's up with you?" she asked with a smile on her face.

"Shhh. He's still asleep. Close the door to my room." I answered her and stepped into the hot shower. "You will never believe this when I tell you what happened."

"Try me." She said leaning up against the door to my bedroom.

"Payne Williams showed up in my classroom last night." Susan stood with her arms across her chest with a look of disbelief on her face.

"You did not fall into bed with him!" She said as her voice rose.

"Shhh. I'd rather get out of here without him being fully awake. He was in town meeting with superiors at the ATF. They're transferring him here. We had dinner and came back here."

"You are kidding me right! You are crazy. Chelsea you can't be serious about getting involved with him again. He is the most unreliable crazy person I have ever met! Not only that but you know he was unfaithful to you when you dated last time. What makes you think he'll be faithful again?"

She was raising very valid points, but it was something I couldn't think about at this time. After the day was over and I had more sleep than a short nap, I could think about the consequences of what I had done. I had no idea what was going on inside Payne's mind. I knew I had to play it cool.

"Listen. I'm going to play this really cool. I have a meeting at school before classes. I'm going to leave him my card and let him decide where he wants to go with this. I have a book signing in Philly next weekend and I'll see where that leads us. Look Suz, he knows I'm not looking for anything right now. The book is taking off and I need time for promotions."

"I just don't want to see you get hurt again. It took so long for you to pick up the pieces last time. Years, if you think about it. Steve just moved out in June. Are you really ready for this?"

"I don't know, but I'll take it one step at a time. I know you care. Just trust my judgment on this one." I told her as I turned off the shower and dried off. Susan jumped into the shower.

"For God's sake do not tell Tommy about this. I'll see you after work." I said as I headed into the bedroom with my robe on and a towel on my head.

I walked into my bedroom to find Payne awake. He had his suit pants on and was in midst of putting on his shirt when I walked in from my shower.

"Sorry. I didn't mean to wake you," I said rushing over to the dressing table. "I've got a faculty meeting this morning at seven that I'm going to be late for if I don't move it. Listen take your time getting ready to go. I know you're not a morning person. Susan is in the shower now but she gets ready in her room. You should be good to shower if you want after she's done."

"If it's all the same, I'll just head back to the hotel and grab a shower there. I'd rather not wrestle with Susan this morning. I know she's not my biggest fan. It would be best if just slipped out."

I had moved to the dresser and picked out my bra and panties and a pair of socks. I moved to the closet next. "I think I am in Philly next weekend if you want to get together. I'm signing at the

Barnes and Noble downtown on Saturday at noon but I have the rest of the weekend free." I turned my back to him and put my thong on. While my back was turned I dropped my robe and grabbed my brown pants to put them on.

"Nice tattoo," he commented. "When did you get that?" I had forgotten about the tattoo. It was a small dagger above my right butt cheek. I paused putting on my bra. I grabbed a short-sleeved cream turtleneck out of my closet.

"I got it for my twenty-second birthday right after graduation. It seemed appropriate at the time." I was hoping he wouldn't read into the design. I threw on a pair of short brown boots and the matching brown suit jacket. I sat down at the vanity table to do my hair. I quickly brushed it out and put it up in a twist with two hair sticks.

I grabbed a purse off the vanity and dug through it. "Here's my business card. It has my personal cell phone number on it as well as my business e-mail. Give me a call before next weekend and we can have dinner or something. I'm taking Amtrak down to Philly after class next Friday, and I usually stay at the Marriott. Building up the points for that vacation."

I went over to the bed and handed him my card. I bent down and kissed him quickly, "Sorry about rushing off like this. I really have to get a move on it. Thanks for last night. I missed you." I kissed him again and then half ran out the door.

CHAPTER 5

She was gone and I was left wondering at her rush. Was it really the meeting or just the awkwardness of the morning after? It was almost six when I had my socks and shoes on and was searching for my tie. Chelsea had never had problems with the morning. I remembered many times in college I had stumbled into her room at two in the morning after the bars closed. I would snuggle up to her and we would end up making love for about an hour. The alarm would then go off at four thiry for her to get to crew practice. It amazed me that she would be able to do that. I was often still asleep when she would return from her workout. I finally found my tie and stuffed the tie in my suit pocket. Smiling at the memory of my tie and the laughter that it had evoked.

I headed down the stairs quietly hoping to not run into Susan. I sure didn't want to stick around for the earful that Susan would give me. That was too much to ask. She was in the kitchen. I had met Susan almost ten years ago at a party at Chelsea's house. She was very blunt about many of the issues in our relationship. She really let me know what she thought of me in college. When we were in a large group, she was polite to me but I knew she was protective of Chelsea.

"Morning Payne," she called to me. "There's coffee if you want it."

I walked hesitantly into the kitchen to grab a cup of coffee. Either she had forgotten her dislike of me or she just didn't care anymore. Probably the latter.

"Good to see you Suz." I said. She poured me a cup of coffee.

"I'm not a real morning person, Payne. The only thing that saves me is coffee." She said as she handed me the cup.

"Chelsea said you're at Time Warner." I said stirring sugar and milk into the cup. I leaned up against the counter.

"Yeah. It's a good job and I like it." She said taking a sip of her coffee. "You're with ATF now?"

"I've been there about four years. They're making me a field manager in New York in about a month." There was no sense in hiding it from her. If things went well this time between Chelsea and I, I might be around more than she would like. "That's why I'm town. I was meeting with superiors about the transfer."

"That's what Chelsea told me this morning. It's good to know that you got your life together." She didn't mince any words. She was very critical of the partying I did in college. There was no denying what I had been in college, but I had changed quite a bit in the last few years.

"Thanks. I like to think that I turned it around." I took my last large gulp of coffee.

"Well, I hope you've turned it around where it comes to Chelsea. She's come a long way since you took off on her. She's not the same naïve girl she once was."

"I know she's not the same person, and I'd like to show her I'm not the same person." I put the coffee cup down in the sink. "Thanks for the coffee Suz. I'm just gonna get my weapon and I'll be on my way."

I walked into the entry way and I opened the front closet. I knew where I stood in New York. It would be an uphill climb if I wanted to make this work with Chelsea. In my gut, I wanted to make it work. I just wasn't sure if it would work in the reality. I grabbed the key off the hook inside the closet door. I pulled down the lock box and got my weapon out. After clipping it back in place, I put the box back on the shelf, hung up the key, grabbed my coat and closed the door.

"By the way," I called to Susan, "Did the Yankees win last night?"

"As a matter of fact they did." She said smiling, "They're doing better than your sorry Phillies."

"I imagine that will be a change moving to New York. I think I'll always be a Phillies and Eagles fan." I put my raincoat on and headed to the door. "See you around Susan."

I walked to the subway thinking about Chelsea and what I could do to convince her I wasn't the same person I was eight years ago. I reached in my coat pocket to pull out my cell phone. I guess I could begin by making her feel appreciated. She would always say I never thought things through. If I remembered her correctly, she loved white roses. I began by calling the hotel and asking for the nearest florist. They passed on a number and I called to order white roses in a vase. Specifically I ordered ten roses. It had been ten years since I had met Chelsea in college and it seemed fitting. I ordered them delivered to Power Memorial High School.

By the time I had ordered the flowers, I was on the subway riding back to Manhattan. Once on the subway, I was thinking about the surprise Chelsea had given me that morning. While the evening was certainly memorable, the tattoo had been a pleasant surprise. I couldn't believe she had gotten the tattoo and the design was very telling. It was identical to the dagger she had bought me from an antique shop. She was the one who had been the history major. She was always into history and was intrigued by the dagger. She said she had been twenty-two when she had the tattoo done. We broke up just before her twentieth birthday. Two years later, she still thought of me. That it was the dagger and not my name wasn't a good thing. The dagger could mean many different things. She obviously didn't hate me. Although if last night was what her hatred contained, I'd gladly take it.

I arrived at the hotel to the reminder of how complicated the move to New York would make my life. I had two cell phone messages and one more message at the hotel from Gina. She had called the hotel trying to reach me when she had not succeeded on my cell. I had turned my cell off after smoking the bummed cigarette. I had quit smoking last year but every once in a while I had one, especially when I was contemplating something very difficult.

I had met Gina about a year and a half after I had moved to Philadelphia. I had begun working with the ATF and would often go out with a few other agents after work on Friday. Gina was in her last year at Temple Law when I met her. When she graduated she took a job with the Philadelphia District Attorney. She was fun to be around but in last six months things had been getting strained between us. Gina wanted to get married soon and I wasn't sure she was the right woman for me. She was very unsure of herself and I was often the target of her uncertainty. She would often call me several times a day to check in with me. For the first time she actually had reason to be distrustful of me.

I hadn't set out to come to New York and look up Chelsea. Things fell into place for a reason. I wasn't quite sure where this would go, but I wanted to give Chelsea and I a second chance. I knew that things with Gina were over a long time ago; it was just easier to continue in the situation that was comfortable. I had planned to make the move to New York the reason for our split. Now, more than ever, it was true.

I arrived at my hotel room and showered. After I showered, I felt like I could take on the conversation with Gina. She answered the phone on the first ring.

"Hey honey." Gina said, "Where have you been?"

"Out with a few of the guys from the New York office. It was a late night and I didn't want to wake you when I got in." The lies were actually painful to tell her but it seemed easier than the truth. It wasn't about Chelsea anyway. It was really about us and how we didn't have a future.

"Listen Gina," I started, "I'm taking the job in New York and it's going to be eating up a lot of my time. I really think we should talk about going our separate ways."

"Payne," she began with a catch in her voice.

"Listen Gina, let's just agree to talk when I get back to Philly. Maybe we can go out for dinner and figure things out."

"OK, but I'm not giving up on us Payne." I winced. I had given up on us a long time ago. I had given up on us when I came to New York to take the new job. I finally gave up on us when I went home with Chelsea last night.

I packed my overnight bag and checked out of the hotel. As I made my way to Penn Station for the train to Philadelphia, I passed a bar that reminded me of the bar where I had met Chelsea.

I had gone out to the Seagrape, a popular Fairfield University bar. I remember it was crowded that night and the crowd was really out of control. I was making my way to the back of the bar when I felt a tug at my shirt.

"I need a blocker," she said. "If you could move to the back I'd love it. I so have to pee."

I glanced over my shoulder and barely saw her, but I did what she asked. I walked all the way to the bathroom and deposited her there. "Thanks," she called out as she went into the bathroom. I went and found my friends at their usual spot.

"You will never believe what just happened to me. Some girl grabbed me from behind and had me block for her all the way to the bathroom." I laughed and sat down.

Next thing I knew she was back. She sat down across from me with two shots of Jose Cuervo Gold, at the time, her drink of choice.

"Thanks for the block," she said. "Want a shot?"

Never one to turn down free alcohol, I grabbed the shot and threw it back. I reached for my beer to chase it and she held my hand not allowing me to chase it. She had tossed her shot back and said, "Just let it burn all the way down."

To this day the sight and smell of Jose Cuervo Gold makes me think of her.

It didn't take long to find out about her. She introduced herself. We were both freshman at the time and with upperclassmen as friends had great fake ID. The Seagrape was always very difficult to get into. You needed to either have excellent fake ID or actually be twenty-one. I soon found out that she was only seventeen while I was almost nineteen. She had a late November birthday while I had done an extra year in kindergarten. I was playing soccer while she was on Crew. We both had demanding schedules but hit it off almost immediately.

Ten years later, I knew something was still there with her. Last night was evidence of that. We needed to see if time would make it possible for us to make it work this time around. I hoped that things would work out and I knew that I had to make an effort. The white roses would be a nice start.

Before I knew it I was at Penn Station and boarding the Amtrak to Philadelphia. I reached into my overnight bag and pulled out Chelsea's book. As I began reading it, I was a little shocked at the main character. I recognized a lot of myself and her grandfather in the lead detective. He was a gritty NYPD detective who didn't take no for an answer. As I noticed in the first chapter, he loved to drink. It reminded me of myself in college. She had said that she had started writing it in college. I knew for certain there were traces of me in the main character. I had to ask her about the coincidences when I saw her next week. It was only ten days away but I would have to set things up.

I took out her business card and my cell. I called her cell knowing I would get her voicemail.

"Hi. You've reached Chelsea Michaels. Please leave your name, number and the best time to reach you. Thanks."

"Hey Chelsea. I just wanted to leave you my number so that you could get in touch with me about next weekend. I'd love to take you out to dinner on Friday night when you get to town. Give me a call next week and we'll set something up. I'm starting to read your book and still hoping for a signing. Talk to you soon."

CHAPTER 6

I was just heading into the Faculty Lounge at Power Memorial High School when I was summoned to the main office. I was pleasantly surprised when I saw the white roses in the front office. The envelope read Chelsea Michaels.

"Who are the flowers from?" Mrs. Linden, the school secretary asked.

I knew right away that they were from Payne. Ten years ago, I loved white roses and he knew that. I opened the card to find "Thank you for the best night in ten years. One rose for each year since we met. I'll call you soon. Payne." Sure enough I quickly counted the roses and found only ten instead of the customary twelve.

"Well?" Mrs. Linden said as I smiled.

"An old friend that I ran into last night." I said and turned to take the roses to my classroom. I sat down at my desk and thought about what the roses meant. Either he was feeling guilty or he really had changed.

White roses. Payne and I had been dating almost a year when someone asked me in front of him what my favorite flower was. White roses, I said. He had mistakenly told me the story of an old girlfriend who had demanded he show up at her house with six red roses for their six-month anniversary. Stupidly he had shown up with the flowers in hand to find her with another guy. I told him that I didn't expect that much. I just wanted one white rose when it came time for our one-year anniversary. He had failed to do that and in the second year of our dating I had not let him forget it. When we said our last good-bye he had taken the time to purchase that one white rose for me.

When the day ended, I turned on my cell phone. For the second time that day, Payne pleasantly surprised me. I immediately saved his phone number into my phone and thought about how next weekend was going to play out. Dinner sounded like a good start as well as a way to gage what would come when he moved to New York. I was still a little uneasy about what our relationship included and where it would go. Susan's words of warning ran through my brain.

Payne had cheated before. Did that mean he would cheat again? When Payne had left Fairfield at the end of our sophomore year, he moved back home and resigned himself to living at home and commuting to St. Francis University. I tried to get down to see him a few times that summer. Between working and training for the crew team, I didn't have a lot of time. The distance was a problem. The fact that I was still at our old school was a problem. When the fall of junior year came, he was trying to make up for lost time; he was trying to fit into his new school. This meant new friends. One of his new friends was a girl from one of his classes. Tracey soon became more than his friend. When I found out about Tracey, I needed proof of what I thought was going on. I borrowed a friend's car and headed out to his parents' house. He was home when I got there, but had planned to go out later that night with Tracey. That was the weekend things ended between us; eight long years ago.

It was the longest five-hour drive back to Fairfield. I was so much in love with Payne at the time. He made me laugh when I couldn't laugh. I was always very self-conscious about my body and he made me feel comfortable in my own skin. What I hadn't realized at the time was how dependent I was on him. In the year after Payne and I broke up, I spent much of my time working hard at school and in crew. In the first six months, I had spiraled into a deep depression and was in counseling to deal with the traumatic turn in my life.

While I went out regularly with my friends and tried to date a few different guys, nothing really developed into a serious relationship. It took me about two years to become intimate with anyone after Payne. The fact that I wouldn't fall into bed with a guy made more than one date with any guy very difficult. By the time I graduated from Fairfield, it was common knowledge on campus that it wasn't worth the effort to try to date me. I was a great friend but nothing more than that.

After college, I dove into work and my master's degree. There wasn't much time to do anything during those first three years out of college. I would teach all day, take evening classes, and then find time for an occasional night out. After my master's degree was completed and I was established as a credible teacher, I began working earnestly on my book. It served as therapy for me. I dealt with Payne and I dealt with my grandfather's illness and death while writing the book.

In the last year, I had finally gotten involved with another guy. My brother had a friend from college who had finished going to medical school. Steve was finally beginning his residency and he needed a place to live that was close to east side of Manhattan. He moved into the basement apartment and lived there until June. He had been offered a practice in Boston and relocated there. Our relationship had convenience for me. He was often too busy to hover but would make time for me when I wanted to go out. He had wanted me to move up to Boston, but I didn't have enough invested in the relationship to leave an established teaching career and the success with the book deal. We still kept in touch via e-mail and I was sure to run into him when he was visiting Tommy.

Now Payne was back in my life. I was a different person than I was in college. In college, I put up with so much more in a relationship than I did now. I wasn't settling for anything. If I could just keep that in mind when I dealt with Payne, I would be OK. Despite his two peace offerings of flowers and the phone call, I was sill apprehensive of talking to him. I waited until the Tuesday before I went to Philly to call him.

I was more than a little nervous when I dialed his cell phone number. It rang once and he picked up.

"Williams." He said.

"Hi Payne. It's Chelsea." I said pacing around my bedroom. When I get nervous, I can hardly stand still.

"Hey. I had all but given up on you." He said, "Are you still coming to town this weekend?"

"I sure am. I want to thank you for the flowers. That was totally unnecessary but very sweet." I was on my third lap of the bedroom.

"How many circles have you walked in?" he asked with a laugh.

I stood still. "I'm not pacing."

He just laughed. "Sure you're not. So when are you coming down?"

"I'm jetting out of school and getting on the three thirty Amtrak out of Penn Station." I started walking again. "That gets me in at almost five."

"How about dinner on Friday night? I'll give you a call Friday morning and meet you at your hotel. Are you staying at the Marriott?"

"Yes through Sunday morning."

"Good. The Marriott isn't too far from my office. I'll see you Friday then."

"Sounds fine." I said and stopped pacing.

"Hey Chels?" He said laughing.

"Yeah."

"How many miles did you just walk in our short phone conversation?"

"Very funny. I'll see you Friday night."

I hung up the phone and sat down on my bed. It had been a difficult week getting to sleep every night. I would keep remembering the night we had spent in bed. I was closing my eyes remembering the unbelievable night when I heard the front door open and my brother Tommy call out to me. "Chelsea? Are you home?"

"Yeah. Be down in a minute."

I went down to see Tommy and was surprised to see his wife and two kids with him. Tommy was six feet five and an easy two hundred fifty pounds. He had the appearance of a firefighter. He always had. He hadn't planned to be a firefighter. Life just kind of turned out that way. He actually had a degree in economics from Fordham University. After trying to find a job in his field, he took the fire exam and easily made it into the academy. He had worked his way up in rank to become a captain in the wake of September eleventh. So many of the firefighters who were eligible for retirement after September eleventh took the retirement incentive.

"Hey guys!" I called as I came down the stairs. It was almost six. I had just come home from the gym and I could smell the pizza in the kitchen. "And you brought pizza!"

I hugged my niece and nephew as they headed down the hall to the kitchen with their mother Julie. Tommy was left putting coats away in the hall closet. I gave him a kiss and immediately asked, "What brings you to Queens at this time of night?"

"I don't know. You tell me." Tommy said with his arms crossed in front of him.

"No wonder Suz went out after work with Joe." I turned and walked away into the living room. "So she told you even after I told her not to tell you."

"Actually she didn't tell me anything. She told me that I needed to come and check up on you." He sat down on the couch and Julie came in with a beer for him and one for me. "So what's up?"

"I'm going to Philadelphia this weekend for a book signing." I started and then took a swig of the Carlsberg. "I'm having dinner with Payne Williams." There I said it.

Tommy's eyebrows drew down and he looked down at his hands. Julie wasn't as diplomatic.

"What the hell are you doing that for?" Julie asked.

"Last week he was in town and he stopped into school to see me. We had dinner and talked. He invited me to dinner while I'm in Philadelphia. It's not a big deal."

Tommy still had his head down. I continued, "He's being transferred to New York with the ATF."

Tommy looked up at that. "He actually finished school and got a job?"

"Really Tommy that's not fair. He was really young and stupid then."

"So what is he now? Almost thirty and stupid? Does he know what happened after he left?"

"No. We haven't had that much time to talk. Probably this weekend there will be more time."

"Did you sleep with him?" Julie asked.

"Not that it matters, but yes." I answered.

Tommy got up and started toward the kitchen. "I don't want to know about that. What is it you say, TMI. Too much information." He turned at the kitchen door and said, "Chels, you're a big girl now. Be careful." He disappeared into the kitchen with the kids.

I sat down on the couch. Julie sat down next to me.

"You know how hard it was for him. He's very protective of you. He had a really tough time dealing with your depression after Payne left. It took all he had not to get in the car and go beat the shit out of him."

"I know Julie. No one knows more than me how bad it was after Payne left. I was the one who took the overdose of sleeping pills. I was the one who had to go into counseling and take antidepressants for a year. Can we all agree that I am a different person now?"

"Yes." Julie said quietly.

"And if I'm a different person is it possible that Payne is a different person?"

She just nodded. "I need you to let me do this and trust my judgment. I'm being very cautious this time. He sent me roses and called me the next day." Julie looked up at me in surprise. "Not like the old Payne is it? How about the fact that I didn't call him back until today." Again she looked at me in surprise.

When Payne and I were a couple, relationships were new to me. I had a brief relationship in high school that went nowhere. I had never had sex before Payne. I fell head over heels in love with him. I worked so hard at our relationship that Payne didn't have to. He almost never called me. I almost always called him. When he ended our relationship I spiraled into a deep depression. It was the height of the fall rowing season. I didn't have time to really think about anything but rowing and school. The problem was the insomnia I had always battled was back in full force. I was getting between two to four hours of sleep. I began taking sleeping pills to help me fall asleep. One night I had taken two sleeping pills with a beer only to be awakened by a fire drill at one in the morning. I then took another two pills with a second beer and couldn't wake up when the second fire drill went off. Fairfield called it an accidental overdose, ordered me into counseling, and put me on probation.

My parents and brother were a little more upset with the incident. It was a very raw spot with them. I went from being a very outgoing young woman to a very quiet introspective woman. Part of my therapy was writing and it became a release for me.

"Jules," I started, "really I am being very cautious. You have to trust me. I'm being careful. I hated who I was eight years ago and I will never allow myself to get there again. No one could ever drive me to that place again, because I won't let myself get there."

She nodded her head. "OK but don't expect Tommy or your parents to come around any time soon. Just take it really slow." She got up and pulled me with her into the kitchen for pizza.

CHAPTER 7

❈

I arrived home at my apartment in Philadelphia to find Gina camped out. I had no doubt in my mind that she had been there since I had gotten off the phone with her. Instead of having a chance to get my bearings before I confronted her I was forced to dive into ending the relationship.

I walked in the front door and headed down the narrow corridor to the living room. Gina was sitting on the maroon leather couch I had just purchased. She was watching Court TV.

"Hi." She said. "Do you want to tell me what's going on because I've been sitting here for the last two hours trying to figure out what the hell went wrong?"

"Gina really. I just got in the door. Let me put my bags down." I said as I walked past her into the bedroom. I dropped my bags on the floor and headed to the closet to lock up my gun. A priority since I knew the conversation was going to go downhill quickly.

She followed me into the bedroom and stood at the door with her arms crossed over her chest. Her blond hair was pulled back into a ponytail and she had on a pair of jeans with an orange sweater.

"If you want to know what went wrong, all you have to do is notice where you are. Instead of waiting for me to get home, unpack, change and call you, you let yourself in here and camped out waiting to ambush me. That's where we went wrong."

"What do you mean?" She became belligerent. "Are you saying I'm where we went wrong?"

"No." I said, "WE are where we went wrong. We're not a good match for each other. You want to hover and spend every minute of the day with me and I need my own space. My own identity. I'm moving to New York in six weeks. Until then I'll be going back and forth between here, New York and Boston. Between training my replacement, packing, and traveling, I don't think I'll have the time to be what you need in your life. Why don't you just cut your losses and move on?"

I had always been a very direct person. I knew this day was coming. The last three months our relationship had become more and more strained. She had wanted to spend more and more time together. She had wanted to move in with me. The reverse was going on with me. I found any reason to spend more time at work. I volunteered for extra days and for out of town seminars. I was pulling away while she was homing in.

"Well isn't that just wonderful. Two years of my life down the drain. Excuse me while I walk away from this less than happy. Just remember honey, I don't break up and make up. This is it. I'm out of here, and you'll realize what you're missing too late." She turned to leave and walked down the hall. She called back at the apartment door and said, "I'll stop by when you're not here to get any stuff I left here. Goodbye Payne."

I heard the door slam. I sat down on the bed thankful she left when she did. It actually went better than I thought it would have. Six Weeks. I could avoid her for six weeks. I had been avoiding her for the last three months. She just hadn't seen it.

The weekend proved to be long and time consuming. I put an ad in the paper to sublet my apartment. I began gathering boxes to pack. Jim Collins, one of the guys at ATF had a guys night out party for me on Saturday night. It was a fun night out at a Phillies game. We had excellent seats in the restaurant level that was behind home plate. Jim's sister-in-law worked for the Phillies and we had first class all the way. We were at the game when Jim mentioned Gina.

"So I heard you and Gina are over." Jim started. "How did that go?"

I took a swig of my beer and shook my head. Most of the guys knew Gina from hanging out on the weekends or they knew her from the District Attorney's office. After she graduated from Temple Law, she began working for the DA. They saw what she was like when she had an idea in her head. Marrying me was apparently an idea she had gotten into her head.

"It went better than I thought, but New York went better."

"Yeah?" Jim asked. "Is the New York office that much more fun than us?"

"Nothing like that. I'm walking down the street and I bumped into my college girlfriend in the most unlikely place."

"You ran into Tracey in New York? I thought she worked in Pittsburgh." He looked puzzled.

"Not Tracey. I forgot you don't know Chelsea."

"Chelsea?"

"Chelsea Michaels. You know *The Hiding Place*."

"No shit. The author?"

"Yeah. She went to Fairfield University with me for two years. She teaches at a private school in Manhattan. I was wandering around Manhattan trying to figure out the move when I saw her book in the window of a Barnes and Noble."

"Get out. You lucky bastard. Was she that hot in college?"

I just smiled.

"Have you read her book?" Jim asked.

"Not yet. She's coming to town next weekend for a book signing."

"I'm there. It's really a well-written book. It's like she's in the business."

"Her grandfather was NYPD for thirty-five years. He worked with it on her until he died about three years ago."

"Any prospects there?"

"Yeah. I'm hoping."

Jim ordered two more beers and smiled, "You sure are one lucky bastard. A promotion, ditching Gina, and picking up a new hottie like Michaels." He toasted me and drank. "Are you going to see her this weekend?"

"I planned to." I said with a smile.

Sunday I laid low and packed up some boxes. I had heard through the grapevine that Gina was slamming me every chance she got. I went out to catch the Eagles game with friends trying not to think about the fact that Chelsea hadn't returned my call.

The new week brought more work and training. I was a little puzzled by the silence from Chelsea. I wasn't sure what that meant. The Chelsea I knew in college would have returned the call. The Chelsea I knew in college was obviously gone.

I had given up on Chelsea and was sitting in a parked car with Jim doing surveillance when my phone rang. I answered it quickly because I was on the job. I also didn't look at the caller-id.

"Williams." I said.

"Hi Payne. It's Chelsea." She said. I was genuinely surprised.

"Hey. I had all but given up on you." I said, "Are you still coming to town this weekend?" Jim perked up on that comment. He seemed more excited than me.

"I sure am. I want to thank you for the flowers. That was totally unnecessary but very sweet." She sounded nervous to me and I was curious if the old Chelsea was really gone or if she was at all the same. When she was in college, she would pace around in a circle when she was nervous. I saw her do it once when she had gotten a speeding ticket on the way back up to school from break. She had arrived at her dorm and was terrified to tell her mother. When she called home, her mother picked up the phone. She immediately began walking in circles trying to calm her nerves while on the phone with her mom.

"How many circles have you walked in?" I asked with a laugh.

"I'm not pacing." She said with a little too much feeling.

I just laughed. "Sure you're not. So when are you coming down?"

"I'm jetting out of school and getting on the three thirty Amtrak out of Penn Station. That gets me in at almost five."

"How about dinner on Friday night? I'll give you a call Friday morning and meet you at your hotel. Are you staying at the Marriott?"

"Yes through Sunday morning."

"Good. The Marriott isn't too far from my office. I'll see you Friday then."

"Sounds fine."

"Hey Chels?" I said laughing.

"Yeah."

"How many miles did you just walk in our short phone conversation?"

"Very funny. I'll see you Friday night."

I hung up the phone and Jim was beside himself with the anticipation of possibility meeting Chelsea. It was all he could talk about for the next hour.

"Where are you taking her for dinner?" Jim asked.

"Like I'd tell you so that you can show up book in hand wanting an autograph."

"Shut up. I'd rather make sure you have the right dinner date set up so that I can get her autograph when she's permanently around."

"I thought casual on Friday night and then maybe a nice dinner on Saturday with a concert."

"Sounds good. The Capital Grille should be good for Saturday night. What time is she arriving Friday?"

"Around five. What do we have going on Friday?"

"Nothing much. We should be done by then. I'll give you dinner with her but I'm calling you to see where you're going after that."

"Fine. Don't make a fool out of me. I have a lot of fences to mend with her. And for the love of God don't mention Gina."

CHAPTER 8

❀

The rest of my week leading up to the trip to Philadelphia was busy and tense. I wasn't sure I had convinced Tommy and Julie I was making good decisions. Susan avoided me Wednesday and Thursday. She made sure she was up and out before I was or she stayed at her fiancé's apartment. It was a wise decision due to the interrogation I received at the hands of my brother and Julie. Before I knew it Friday arrived. I packed carefully; something casual and something dressy for each day. School seemed to fly by. I had assigned an in class essay to avoid having anything pressing to tend to during that day and then plenty to grade for the train ride to and from Philadelphia.

Before I knew it, I was hailing a cab to Penn Station and heading down the escalator to the Amtrak level. Amtrak is notorious for being late, but surprisingly the train was on time, not very crowded and actually enjoyable. I was nervous about the weekend. I didn't want to come on too strong, but at the same time I was afraid of not showing enough interest. There was no doubt in my mind that what I felt for Payne had never gone away. Where we would go from here was anyone's guess. During the hour and half train ride I decided I was going to have fun and if the relationship progressed that was great, if not at least I was having fun.

The train pulled into the station and I grabbed a cab to the Marriott. When I got there, I checked in. Waiting at the counter for me was an envelope. I walked up to my room and opened it. It was from Payne.

> Chelsea,
> I'm going to be stuck at work until about five thirty or six. Here are the spare keys to my apartment. Have the concierge call you a cab. It's about a ten-block walk. I'll meet you there at around 6:30. Sorry about this. We had a tip on a small stash of weapons and need to investigate. I'll make it up to you.
> Payne.

As much as I should have been angry with this, I had to be impressed. A similar situation happened in college. Payne was two hours late meeting me out. Rather than it being anything work related, Payne had been hanging out drinking with a few buddies and had lost track of the time. I had been left waiting for him out at the Seagrape. He eventually showed up two hours late with no explanation and no remorse. That he took the time during the day to drop off the note and keys to his apartment greatly impressed me. He could have left me waiting in my hotel room.

I quickly showered and put on a pair of jeans, short black boots and a low cut black shirt. I had dressed to kill. I have always been well endowed and as a high school and then even college student, I was always hiding two of my best assets: my breasts. Teaching in an all boys' school, I never wore low cut shirts. I had purposely packed this shirt that I purchased at Susan's urging this summer. It seemed the perfect time to finally wear it. I grabbed my jacket and headed through the lobby.

It was actually a fairly warm mid-October evening and I had the concierge hail me cab. It was a short ride down the Philadelphia streets to reach Payne's apartment. Armed with his spare keys, I let myself into the building, an old warehouse converted into one and two bedroom apartments. I easily found his apartment on the fourth floor. I was about to put the key in the lock when the door opened. Expecting Payne to be at the door, I was shocked to see an attractive blonde.

"Sorry." I said. I looked down at the note to check the apartment number. I realized I had the right number. "Sorry I was looking for Payne Williams."

"He's not here right now. Can I help you?" She asked

"I'm sorry. I'm Chelsea Michaels, a friend of his from New York." I held out my hand to her. She reluctantly shook my hand. "He left me a note that he was running late and that I should meet him here."

"That would be fine except that most of the apartment is packed or covered in boxes right now. I was just waiting for him to get home to see what he wanted me to pack up next. Are you staying close by?"

"At the Marriott." I was beginning to feel uncomfortable. She quite obviously lived here with Payne. That made me a little on the angry side. I guess Payne hadn't changed all that much. "Well just tell him I stopped by." I turned to leave and decided to leave the keys with her.

"Here are the keys he leant me. Tell him I said thanks." I turned and walked away feeling very betrayed.

I was walking down the street headed back to the Marriott a little angry and sad. I was saddened due to the turn in events that obviously meant that Payne and I had no future. I was angry for being made to look the fool in front of what quite obviously was his girlfriend. I returned to my room and put on my silk pajamas. The Rangers were actually playing the Flyers tonight. I found the game on TV, ordered room service and took out my laptop. I was under pressure from my agent and publisher to write another book. I dove into writing hoping that I would cool off.

CHAPTER 9

❀

It was almost six thirty when I arrived at my apartment Friday night. I was excited to see Chelsea. Earlier that morning we had received a tip about an apartment just over the border in Camden, New Jersey that had a weapons stash. On the way out to Camden, I stopped at the Marriott and scribbled a note for Chelsea to meet me at my apartment and threw the spare set of keys Gina had just dropped off at my office two days before. I hopped in the car with Jim.

"This better go quickly." I said to him. We drove to Camden and found a small arsenal of rifles and assault weapons in an apartment. Unfortunately, the tip had panned out. After confiscating the unregistered guns, we headed back to the office to fill out the paperwork that accompanied a raid of this proportion. At around five forty-five, Jim threw me out of the office to head home.

I walked into the building and headed up to the fourth floor. When I walked into the apartment, it was dark. No Chelsea. That was odd. Maybe Amtrak was late as usual. I picked up the phone and called the front desk.

"Has Chelsea Michaels checked in yet?" I asked.
"Yes sir."
"Did she receive the envelope I left for her?"
'There's nothing at the desk for her."

"Can you transfer me up to her room?" I asked turning on the light in the dining area.

"She's not receiving calls at this time." He said. This puzzled me. As he said this, I turned to see the envelope with the keys on the dining room table.

"Thanks." I said, hanging up. I walked over to the table. Next to the envelope and keys was a note.

> Payne,
> I was here packing up my stuff when your friend stopped by. She said thanks anyway.
> Gina

"Crap." I said. I grabbed my coat and headed out the door. Chelsea had to have shown up while Gina was here and drawn a very bad conclusion. "Shit. Shit. Shit" I said as I briskly walked down the street toward the Marriott. I pulled out my phone and called Jim.

"Hey." Jim answered. "I didn't expect to hear from you for a while."

"Well things are all screwed up here. Apparently Gina was at my apartment when Chelsea arrived. Lord only knows what she said to her. Chelsea left and I'm off to the Marriott to do damage control. Considering Chelsea didn't know about Gina last week when I was in New York, I'll probably spend the rest of the night maybe weekend digging myself out of a hole."

"Flowers man. Stop and pick up flowers." Jim said. "Good luck."

I hung up and did as he suggested. I grabbed a bunch of flowers from the main lobby gift shop and headed over to the front desk. This was where I was going to play hardball. I took out my badge

"I need Chelsea Michaels' room number."

"Certainly." The girl behind the counter said, "Room three twenty-seven. She has a room service order arriving shortly."

I made my way up to her room and was pleasantly surprised to have something work out well that day. I showed the waiter my badge and waited as he knocked, letting her know her room service was there. I tipped him and waited with the tray.

She opened the door to find me standing with one hand behind my back and the other balancing the tray of food. She was wearing navy blue silk pajamas with a matching silk robe.

"Room service. Did you give up on me?" I said with a smile. "I heard you had a run-in with my ex."

Her arms were folded across her chest. "You don't have a date with her to pack?"

"Not on your life." I said, "She was there grabbing a few last things and must have recognized her old keys in your hand. Hence the total bitchiness. Can I come in to discuss this with you?" I produced the flowers as an apology.

"I guess so." She said moving out of the doorway and walked further into the room. I followed her into the room and put the tray down on the small table.

"Nice room" I said sitting down in the chair. "You should let me book your rooms. I get a government rate."

She didn't look too thrilled with me. She sat down on the king size bed and waited for the explanation.

"OK. Here goes. I started dating Gina about two years ago. The last six months have been a steady decline. I knew the promotion and transfer were coming soon and I figured it would be easier to end our relationship when I moved to New York. I saw you on Thursday night and I ended things with Gina that next day. This week she came by my office and dropped off her keys, which I left for you at the front desk. I think she probably conned the super into letting her into the apartment."

She was silent after I finished. She put her head down in her hands. I got up out of the chair and knelt down in front of her. I pulled her hands away from her face to see the tears I knew were there. I sat down next to her and pulled her onto my lap. She was crying very softly. I stroked her back and held her.

"I'm sorry." I said to her. "I'm so sorry." I kissed the top of her head. She continued to cry silently for another minute. I kept stroking her arms through the navy silk robe.

"It was like Tracey all over again, Payne. There she was in your apartment not letting me in. She hinted at the fact that you and she were packing together and moving to New York. It took all I had to turn and walk away from your apartment without either breaking down or killing her. I walked all the way back to the hotel I was so angry. I felt like the biggest fool. I could hear the "I told you so" of Tommy and Susan all the way back. I was so angry with you. I broke a sweat walking home."

"Tommy knows about us?" I asked with surprise.

"Yeah he confronted me about it on Tuesday evening. He and Julie were full of warnings to not let you take advantage of me; warning me to not spiral into depression again."

I pulled her chin up to look into her eyes. There was an anger and puzzled look in my eyes. "What happened after we ended? Suz hinted it went badly for you."

She shook her head and looked down in her lap. I tilted her face up again to look at me. "Chelsea. I want to make this work. You have to believe me, but we need to put the past in the past. I need to know so I can handle it in New York."

She nodded, looked down a her lap and began quietly, "I wasn't sleeping. I had crew and school. I was taking three upper level histories and a couple of education classes. I needed my sleep. One night in October I took two sleeping pills with a beer. The fire alarm woke me up. I went outside and came back in to take two more pills with another beer. The second alarm went off and I never woke up. They brought me to the hospital and pumped my stomach. The college put me on probation. I missed Head of the Charles that year. I had mandatory counseling and began taking anti-depressants. It was about a year before the doctors thought I could come off the meds. It was ugly. Tommy was crazy when he found out about it. My mom cried for about a month. I finally pulled out of it just after my twenty-frist birthday."

She stopped and looked up at me. "I'm so sorry." I said to her. I hugged her to me. "I'm so very sorry. Shit. I knew I had a lot to make up to you but I had no idea it was this much."

"I had better years than that one." She said with a smile. She looked up at me and kissed my mouth. "I want to make this work Payne, but I'm scared."

She began to kiss me again slowly. It didn't take much to make me want her. She was sitting on my lap in a king size bed in a hotel room. I was more than a little aroused since she opened the door in her silk pajamas. I immediately felt the blood rushing to my groin. Her hair had been pulled up into a ponytail when she answered the door but she was still sexy. I began to push the robe off her shoulders to get at her pajama top. She was just as eagerly pulling at my golf shirt.

"Sorry no tie tonight." I said with a laugh. I unclipped my gun and phone putting them on the nightstand. I was in a hurry to get her shirt unbuttoned. The silk was rubbing against her breasts making her nipples hard. She wasn't wearing a bra underneath. I rolled her to her back and began to stroke her breasts. She began pulling at my pants. I moved in small kisses down her stomach to the drawstring pajama pants. I pulled out the ties with my teeth. I could smell the Chanel Number Five that she always wore. It was driving me insane. My penis was so hard at this point that when she reached in my pants to touch the head of it I almost came in her hand. I tore her pants off her to find that she had no panties on underneath. I rolled her over onto her stomach. I quickly plunged into her.

She cried out with a moan. The original urgency disappeared and I slowed down to a steady pace with Chelsea on her knees grabbing the spread of the bed in her hands. She began making the noises that I had always loved to hear. I reached around and began to massage her closer to her orgasm. She was wet and swollen with need. I continued to push into her from behind while rubbing her into a slick frenzy. She was moaning into the pillow and grabbing at the spread. I was caressing the dagger tattoo above her hip and had just come completely out of her. She moaned in protest as I rolled her over and again slid inside her. I was moving in her slowly when my cell phone rang.

Knowing that so much could still go wrong with the raid from earlier that day, I grabbed it and collapsed on top of her. I looked at the caller id. It was Jim. She was writhing in pleasure. I put my other thumb in her mouth for her to suck on it. She had the most unbelievable way of making love to my fingers. She would do it while I was sitting next to her, while I was making love to her. Anywhere. I was slowly sinking in and out of her with my thumb in her mouth to try to stifle her cries when I pressed the send button.

"Jim this had better be important." I said slipping out of her slowly. She tightened the walls of her vagina around me and I shuddered.

"You busy?" Jim asked as I sank in again. Chelsea was sucking so hard on my thumb I couldn't pull it out of her mouth. I looked into her eyes as she continued to nip at my fingertips. She lifted her hips and I sank deeper. I could feel her stretching to take my entire length inside her. She was so tight and contracting around me I knew I couldn't keep talking to Jim for much longer.

"You could say that. What's up?" Another push. Another squeeze of her around me. Her hips came off the bed and I pushed really hard. She gasped, lost the hold on my thumb, and moaned.

Jim laughed because he figured out what we were doing. "Just wanted to tell you that a couple of us are headed out to the Penalty Box tonight and we wanted you and Chelsea to join us. But it sounds like you have better plans. Give me a call if that changes."

Chelsea had taken that moment to pull her legs up and wrap them around my back. She had driven her hips up so high and tightened around me I almost came.

"Fine." I said gruffly and hit the end button. She laughed.

"Glad to know I can distract you." She said. But I had the last laugh as I came all the way out of her and then drove into her and she screamed out with the pleasure of having me imbedded all the way inside her. I was suddenly very aware of the fact that I hadn't put a condom on. About six months into our relationship in college, Chelsea went on the pill and we stopped using condoms. I wasn't sure if she was still on the pill and wouldn't make the assumption that she was giving me free license to come inside her. I waited until I was at my breaking point. When I felt the spasms of her orgasm squeeze me into the beginnings of mine, I pulled out of her and came all over her stomach.

I collapsed on top of her the moisture of my sweat and semen between us. Her eyes were wide open in wonder and her breathing was labored. I reached over to the nightstand and grabbed tissues out of the tissue box. I rolled off her and began wiping the semen off her belly. She moaned as I gently wiped the moisture into her. I looked at her face as I caressed her belly and saw her close her eyes in pleasure.

"You like that baby?" I asked surprised at her pleasure in such a simple thing.

"Yes." She croaked out. I continued to wipe at the moisture on her belly and she continued to writhe in pleasure. "Don't stop. It feels so good."

"Yeah?" I sounded surprised. I was no longer wiping up but instead I was caressing her breasts. "You want more?"

"What do you think?" she answered putting her hand around my penis. She began caressing it into its hardened state. She pushed me down onto my back and moved down my body with kisses. She stopped at my nipples and pulled on them with her teeth her one hand was still stroking up and down my penis. The tip was moist already and she put her lips around it and I closed my eyes lost to the sensation of her mouth moving up and down the shaft. She was running her tongue down the tender underside her hands caressing my scrotum. She was increasing her pace and I was thrusting into her mouth with the urgency of the oncoming rush. I could feel myself sink into her mouth deeper until I was actually in her throat. She kept up with my thrusts gasping for breath as I moaned loudly finally giving in to the incredible orgasm. She kept sucking on me as I came into her mouth swallowing everything I poured into her. When there was nothing left. She moved back up to brush the hair away from my forehead. I grabbed her hand and kissed the palm.

"You always had the best mouth." I said. "Do you know I have to turn the Cadillac commercial with Zeppelin's Rock and Roll off when it comes on the TV? I immediately get hard thinking about you on your knees in front of me in your parent's basement."

She laughed. "If it's any consolation, I get wet when I hear that song." I laughed and rolled over. The clock said seven fifty. "Are you up for a night out with my friends? Bars close early here so we won't be too late."

"Sure. I need a shower first if that's OK."
"Sounds good to me." I replied.

CHAPTER 10

I was in the shower thinking about the direction my life was taking. I had never been one to fall into bed with a man. I could count on one hand the number of partners I had in my life and they were fewer than the fingers on my hand. In some ways I was very angry with myself for falling into bed with Payne not once now but twice. In my heart I knew I still loved him, but there was so much more to sort out. As the water beat down on my head and back, I was reminding myself that if things worked out that would be fine if not just have fun.

I heard the bathroom door open and Payne called to me.

"Did you know the Rangers and the Flyers are playing each other tonight?"

"Of course. When things went south at your apartment, I came back here and changed into my pajamas to settle in to watch the game. The first period's almost over by now. Do you want a shower?"

"No. I'm good." Payne said and I turned the water off. "If I got in there now, we'd never get out of the hotel room."

I pulled back the shower curtain and Payne handed the hotel towel to me. He was leaning up against the counter fully clothed smiling. I smiled back as I dried off.

"The phone call before was from Jim. He works with me. He is desperate to meet you. He is a huge fan and will make my last few weeks in Philly miserable if he doesn't get to meet you."

I laughed and stepped out of the tub. He stood there watching me. I looked back at him and asked, "What?"

"Do you want to explain that nice bit of art work above your right butt cheek?"

"Not particularly." I said and walked out into the hotel room. I went to the dresser and pulled out clothes. "Casual right?"

"Chelsea," He warned me, "don't change the subject."

"Right. Of course it's casual. Are we going someplace to watch the game?" I continued ignoring his desire to know about the tattoo. I had a black bra and thong on and was pulling on my jeans when he said my name again.

I looked up at him, as he was moving closer. He had a very serious look on his face. I imagine the look he has when he is pursing someone in the field. He was intent on having this conversation and I was intent on not having it. I had pulled on my jeans and was standing up when he arrived in front of me. We were toe to toe and he was staring down into my eyes.

"Tell me." He said.

"I didn't want to forget." I stepped around him and headed toward the closet. I got as far as the closet door. He shut it and put his hands on either side of me. I leaned my head against the mirrored door. He turned me around and all but pinned me to the door.

"You didn't want to forget what?" he asked. I could tell his patience was running out.

I looked into his intense green eyes. "I didn't want to forget how painful and beautiful love could be."

He lowered his head and kissed me quickly. "I don't want to forget how great things were, but we need to forget all the hurt and move on."

"So get out of my way, let me finish getting dressed and we can go meet your friends." He took his arm away. I reached inside the closet and pulled out a simple black shirt and my black boots. I finished putting on my clothes and threw my damp hair up in a twist. Payne lay on the bed watching me. I was a little unnerving to have someone watching your every move. I grabbed the case I used for my toiletries. I began taking things out to reach the lipstick I had thrown in there earlier. I came across my bottle of Chanel Number 5 and sprayed in on me. Finally I had found the lipstick. I quickly put it on and started putting things back in the bag.

"Are you still on the pill?" Payne asked me. I made eye contact with him in the mirror.

"Yes." I said as I put the pill case back into the bag. I turned around and he smiled at me.

"Are you ready to go?" he asked getting up from the bed.

"Don't even get an attitude with me about getting ready. It's eight twenty. Any other woman would have you waiting another half an hour. At least."

He stopped in front of me and kissed me. "And they wouldn't look half as good as you."

We walked out the door into the hallway. In the lobby, we grabbed a cab and headed to The Penalty Box. It was about a ten minute drive from the hotel to the bar. It was amazing the difference in Payne. He was very attentive to me. The ride from the hotel to the bar he held my hand. His thumb was stroking my palm. I was looking out the window for most of the ride. I could feel him looking at me.

"What's your friend like?" I asked.

"Jim, he's the one that called. We met at St. Joe's. We interned together at ATF and we both got jobs there. He's fun. He's with ATF but also in the National Guard. He's built like your brother Tommy. He's taller than I am and all muscle."

We got out of the cab. He was at the curb when I got out and he made a comment about my shirt. "Jesus Chelsea! You're practically falling out of that shirt."

I looked down and didn't see anything overly outrageous about my shirt. It was a black v-neck t-shirt that wasn't overly revealing. Sure if I bent over you could see my bra but when I was standing up it was perfectly respectful. I laughed.

I took his hand in mine and walked into the sports bar. It was crowded with Flyers fans. Payne was pulling me through the bar. We moved through the crowd easily to a table next to the bar. The table had three guys sitting at it. When they saw Payne, one guy got up from the table and walked over to Payne. He was about six feet five inches and an easy two hundred pounds. His two hundred pounds were solid muscle. He had the look of a professional football player. He had a clean shaved head. He was laughing as he hugged Payne but I could only imagine what he was like when doing his job.

"Jim," Payne said, "This is Chelsea. Michaels."

I extended my hand out to him. He took it in his and shook it.

"Ma'am it's a pleasure to meet you." Jim said. He had a slight southern accent. He offered me a chair next to him. "I loved your book."

"Glad to hear it. Here's the important question. Do you like the Rangers or the Flyers?" I asked.

"Neither really. I love sports. Hockey is new to me. I follow the Flyers to keep the guys watching my back happy. I prefer football."

"I do too, but I fell in love with the Rangers when they finally won the cup in 94."

"Beer?" Jim asked holding a pint glass up.

I nodded and he poured me a glass. It was a dark larger and when I tasted it I recognized it as Sam Adams.

"Sam Adams. Good choice." I said. I began to drink the beer with an eye on the game on the big screen. The Rangers were down two to one in the third period.

"Payne," Jim said around me. "I don't know how you pulled this one off. She's hot, writes a good cop thriller, loves sports, and knows beer." He paused looked right at me and said, "Sweetheart, if he screws up, I'm still available."

"Jim." Payne warned as I laughed.

"Payne, I need to eat something or I'll be bombed after two beers."

Payne smiled, "Promise? You are so much fun when you're drunk."

I gave him my look of death and he got up to order some food at the bar. Jim took advantage of Payne's absence to talk to me. Every sip he took made his southern accent more pronounced and my New York accent heavier.

"Where are you from Jim?" I asked.

"Atlanta. I went to St. Joe's and stayed up here. I'm surprised you caught that I wasn't from here. You met Payne at Fairfield, right?"

"Yeah. We were both freshman ten years ago. He left after two years. I teach at Power Memorial High School in New York."

"Kareem Abdul Jabbar's high school?"

"Damn you're good with your sports trivia. Not a lot of people know that." I was impressed. I saw Payne making his way back to the table with another pitcher of beer. I was on my second pint and beginning to feel a little buzzed. I hadn't eaten since the pretzel I grabbed in Penn Station.

"You teach at an all boys high school?" Jim asked and when I nodded he made the usual comment I hear about that. "Damn. How come I didn't have any teachers that looked like you in high school."

"I'm sure you did." My usual response to that comment, "You just didn't notice."

"I think I would have noticed someone who looked like you. Listen," Jim said, "before he gets back here. I want you to know he's been looking forward to this weekend all week. He was really bummed we had that raid today. He usually loves a good raid, but it meant he would be late to see you. He's a good man. Give him a shot."

I winked at him and said, "No worries." I finished my second pint as Payne sat down next to me. He had another pitcher with him and some chips from the bar.

"Sorry." He said, "It took me a while to get the bartender's attention. I ordered you a burger. It should be out in about ten minutes. I brought some chips over to tide you over."

"Next time send me. I'll bend over and get faster service."

"Not fair." Payne said. "Her shirt is entirely too low."

Jim sat up straight and looked over my shoulder. "I don't know it could be lower." He winked at me.

"Jim." Payne warned again. I put my hand on his knee and squeezed.

"He's having fun with you." He smiled at me and I ran my hand up his leg.

"Where the hell is that burger?" Payne frowned. He took my hand off his thigh and put it on the table. "You need to eat or this is going to turn into that night at Connolly's in Manhattan." I laughed.

Jim was intrigued. "What happened that night?" He pushed the chips toward me and filled my pint glass again.

I blushed and Payne began the story. "We were out with her brother Tommy and a few of his friends. Tommy had gone home and Chelsea was completely bombed. She was dancing in front of me to AC/DC's 'You shook me'. I put my hand up her shirt and snapped her bra. Her answer to that was to unhook it, take it off, and shove it down my shorts. To my surprise and pleasure she reenacted the Drew Barrymore incident on the Letterman Show."

Jim's jaw dropped while I turned beet red and smacked Payne in the arm.

"You didn't!" Jim finally said.

"Yeah," I said, "I did and the guy at the next table actually saw it. He started telling his friends I had just flashed Payne and they were all staring at me. They were waiting for a repeat performance. I told them it wasn't happening."

"Priceless." Jim said offering his glass to toast me. "You are definitely priceless. Any sisters I could get my hands on?"

"Nope." I smiled and took another drink. Payne had moved his hand to the back of my chair and was rubbing the back of my neck casually. "Payne said you're in the National Guard. Have you seen any action lately?"

"Nah. It's coming soon. I'm not sure when but soon." Jim turned back to the game.

Payne leaned over and whispered in my ear. "Behave yourself. Jim would love the chance to take you away from me." He slipped his tongue in my ear.

I laughed and finished off my third beer. At this point, I was in desperate need of food. I couldn't follow the puck on the ice. That was a bad sign. Just when I thought I was going to have a very drunk evening, my burger arrived. I dove into the burger and fries with gusto.

"I love a woman with a healthy appetite." Jim said watching me eat.

The game was winding down and the Flyers were going to win much to my unhappiness. The crowd was starting to thin out. I was still very buzzed and afraid to get up from the seat. It was almost eleven and I was starting to feel how long the day had been.

Payne could see I was getting tired. He leaned over and whispered in my ear. "Do you want to get going?" He pulled the lobe between his teeth.

I nodded.

"My place."

I nodded again.

"Jim, we're gonna scoot. It's been a long day and Chels has a signing tomorrow. We'll catch you later."

Jim stood up and offered me his hand. He pulled me up out of my chair and gave me a big hug. "I enjoyed meeting you. We'll see you again soon?"

I nodded again. "You come up to New York and I'll show you the town." I gave Jim a quick kiss on his cheek. Payne shook his hand.

Payne took my hand and led me out of the bar. We hopped in a cab and he directed him to his apartment. I sat in the cab with my hand on his knee. I was sliding my hand up and down his leg. Payne put his hand on top of my hand and brought it to his lips. The cab pulled up in front of his apartment building on Market Street and we got out.

We headed up to the fourth floor and down the hall to his apartment. He unlocked the door and for the second time that day I was about to head into this apartment. I paused.

"Come on." Payne said pulling me in the corridor that led into the apartment.

Down the narrow hallway there was a wide-open living room with large windows. There was a red leather couch and a matching chair and ottoman. It was breath taking. Contrary to Gina's statement earlier, there were not boxes everywhere.

"You'll never get this in Manhattan." I said to him. "This is gorgeous!"

He walked into the small kitchen. He opened the fridge. He pulled out a bottle of water and offered it to me. I walked over to him in the kitchen and went to take the water from him. He pulled it up out of my reach. I reached for it. It put me leaning up against him. He brought his arms down around me. He leaned into me against the counter. I could feel his very hard arousal.

"You still hungry." He asked me.

"You know I could really go for some ice cream. Do you have any?" I asked.

He reached up to open the freezer door. "Nah. Just some Otter Pops. You know those long frozen flavored ice."

My eyebrow went up. "Really?" I smiled.

"What's that about?" He asked intrigued.

"Do you remember Jen from college?"

"Your roommate freshman year?"

"Yeah. She and her boyfriend had a little fun with some otter pops once."

Both his eyebrows went up. "Really?" He asked surprised. "She was always so quiet. Huh. I never would have guessed. You want an otter pop?" He said leaning harder into me.

"Show me the rest of the place first." I bent over and took of my boots. He took my hand and led me down the hall to his bedroom. It was small but very nice. There was a queen-size bed with a plain wooden headboard and footboard. There was a maroon comforter with blue stripes and matching curtains. It was simple and very masculine. I sat down on the bed and yawned. Payne grabbed a pair of boxer shorts out his dresser and tossed them to me.

"You look beat." He said. I unhooked my bra and pulled the straps down from inside my shirt. The movement that every woman knew how to do and most men were amazed with had been shown to the world in *Flashdance*. I put it down on the nightstand, took off my black socks, and stood up to take off my jeans. I folded the pants and put on the boxers. I shook my hair out of the twist adding the clip to the pile of clothes

"I need a good night's sleep." I said as I pulled back the covers. "Do you mind?" While I wouldn't have minded making love again, I was so tired I could barely keep my eyes open.

"Babe," Payne said, "if anyone deserves a good night sleep tonight, it is most definitely you. Be my guest." He went back into the living room to shut out the lights. He climbed in bed with me and pulled me up against him.

"I liked your friend Jim." I said with a yawn. "He's funny." I had closed my eyes. Payne was leaning up an elbow and brushing the hair off my forehead.

"Jim adores you." He said kissing my forehead. "I do too."

I smiled and easily fell asleep in Payne's arms.

CHAPTER 11

❀

As much as I would have loved to make love to her again, I knew she needed her rest. She had a big day in the morning. I was happy to just lie there watching her sleep. This was definitely a change for me. Whenever I was in bed with Chelsea, all I ever thought about was making love to her. It had been impossible to sleep in bed with her and not have sex. When I moved on to other women, I thought I would feel the same way. There was always a sexual attraction, but not the desperation of making love. Before I would always give in to the temptation of Chelsea. This had to be one of the few times I ever slept in a bed with her but hadn't had sex. I was content to just watch her.

Usually she was the one who had problems getting to sleep. This time it was me. I was digesting everything that had occurred that night. Gina almost blowing any chance I had with Chelsea. The long walk over to the hotel. Chelsea's confession of the overdose and the hard year that followed was very upsetting for me. I had no idea she had cared that much. I had no idea my selfishness would cause her to sink that low. Amazingly, she had recovered. She could always land on her feet.

I looked down at her sleeping face and realized I wanted her to be around. Forever. I knew she was special. What we had between us was special. Years had gone by and it was still there. I needed to make her trust me. I needed to make her family trust me. I had a very difficult task ahead of me. I knew it. At that moment I started to formulate a plan.

I smiled; bent down to kiss her on her lips and whispered, "I love you."

I thought I saw her smile as I pulled her back into my front. She took my hands in hers and I drifted off to sleep.

I woke up and she was gone. I had slept longer than I had wanted to. It was almost nine when I reached over to feel her side of the bed. On the bedside table was a note.

> Payne,
> I went back to the hotel to get a workout in, shower and change. I'm due at the Barnes and Noble on Walnut Street at eleven thirty. Signings begin at noon. It should last until three. Meet me at the hotel afterwards. Thanks for another wonderful evening.
> Love,
> Chelsea

"Love Chelsea." It was a nice start. I had reservations for dinner tonight at The Capital Grille and tickets to Bizet's *Carmen* at Annenberg Hall. It was the beginning of my plan to make her trust me. Her birthday was the weekend before Thanksgiving and I wanted to do something special for her. I would find out what her plans were for that weekend and build a dazzling weekend around it. It was a little over a month away. I would be in New York full time by then. I needed to succeed by Christmas. That was the plan.

I got out of bed and showered. I wasn't going to wait until after the signing to see her. I wanted to see her at work. I needed to see this other side of her; this new Chelsea that had not been there when we in college. I was sure Jim would be there. I would casually hang out. The place was big enough that I'm sure she wouldn't see me. I needed to pick up some new music and their music department was excellent.

It was ten thirty before I left my apartment. I picked up my car at the office. I checked that everything was fine in connection with Camden raid the day before. I parked my car at work rather than pay for the parking at my apartment building. It was easier. I imagined I would have a problem in New York with my car and parking. The ATF offices were actually in Brooklyn across the East River from Manhattan. I had no desire to actually live in Manhattan and hoped to get a small apartment in Brooklyn that would allow me to leave my car at work. Chelsea's vacant basement apartment was too much of a temptation as well as a hurdle with her family that I didn't need to put in my way. I grabbed my laptop from work and headed for the Barnes and Noble.

There was a decent crowd for her signing. She had a small table set up and copies of her book for people to purchase and her to sign. I skirted the area and headed to the café. There I bought a coffee and settled in with my laptop. I began searching the online apartment listings. There was a new area of Brooklyn that was getting a lot of attention DUMBO (Down Under the Manhattan Bridge Overpass). If you could get past the name, it was great section of the city with terrific views of the Manhattan skyline. Many of the apartments were in buildings similar to mine, but the cost was two to three times the cost of mine. I settled on a small studio apartment to save some money. I was so engrossed in finding an apartment that Jim was able to sneak up on me.

"Hey." Jim said and sat down with me. "How did your night end up last night? Better than the start?"

I laughed. "You called at the best part of my evening, but it turned out really great."

He laughed. "I didn't want to bring that up last night in front of Chelsea. She was already blushing at the drunken strip tease story you told. She embarrasses rather easily. That's gonna be fun if she keeps you around."

"Don't be fooled by her. She has an older brother and mostly guy friends; she can dish it out as well as she can take it. Watch your back. She likes you. She said, 'He's fun.' That means your fair game for her pranks."

"Really? What kind of pranks?"

"One time in college one of the guys on the men's crew team wouldn't stop bothering her. You know how their feet are tied into the boat? She filled this guy's shoes with day old chili. He never bothered her again."

Jim laughed loudly and Chelsea looked over in our direction. She smiled and waved at us. So much for observing quietly. Leave it to Jim to blow my cover. Jim waved back.

"Damn! You are one lucky man. What's your plan?" he asked.

"I've got a short term and long term plan. She needs to trust me again. I need to prove it to her. Long term. I'm gonna marry her." I was looking at her while I told him my plan then I turned to look at him.

Jim was shocked.

"She doesn't trust me right now. I hurt her badly in college. She caught me cheating on her with Tracey. I'll never forget the hurt look in her eyes. She trusted me while I was away from her. I betrayed that trust. Her family pretty much hates me. I'm going to have to kiss their asses to make it work."

Jim whistled low. "I've got to see this. What's your timetable?"

"Christmas." I said firmly. "I need to have it fixed by Christmas. I want a ring on her finger at Christmas. Any suggestions?"

"I don't know man. That's a tall order. But if anyone can make it happen it's you."

"Her birthday is right before Thanksgiving. I've got some plans in mind for that weekend but I need to know where she'll be. If I can work on her that weekend, I'll work on her family Thanksgiving weekend."

"Listen I've got drill the weekend before Thanksgiving and without a doubt I'll probably get orders. Can I come up Thanksgiving weekend and have a wild time in New York City?"

"Sounds like a plan. You're sure about the orders?"

"Yeah. I knew it was only a matter of time. I hope it's not some door opening bullshit detail. I hate that crap. The degree in international relations seemed like such a great idea in college. I really hope they haven't figured that out. If I'm heading over to the sandbox, I had better be able to smash some heads."

I laughed loudly now. Chelsea looked over again at us. Only Jim would look at a door opening diplomatic mission as bullshit. From what he had heard from Army buddies who had done one or more tours in the Middle East, it pretty much sucked. Yet he had the ability to stay out of the line of fire and didn't want to.

I looked over at Chelsea again and noticed that Gina was on line to have her book signed.

"Mother fucker." I said and started to get up. Jim saw what I saw at the same time. By the time we were at the signing table, Gina was already at the front of the line.

"Good to see you again," Chelsea said. "Gina wasn't it."

"Yeah." She said, "Sorry you missed Payne last night."

Chelsea smiled. "No thank you. He actually caught up with me at my hotel room and we had a lovely evening." She handed the book back to her and moved onto the next person who just happened to be Jim.

"Hey Jim." Chelsea said. "I told you I'd sign your copy privately. Don't buy one here. That's what friends are for."

Jim laughed, "Sugar I'm glad I can count you as one of my friends." He skipped the signing and caught up with Gina in the doorway of the store. I saw him grab her by the arm.

"You OK?" I said to Chelsea.

"Yeah." She said picking up the pitcher of water on the table. Her hand was shaking. I put my hand on top of hers and smiled at her.

"I'm out of this city in five weeks and I'll never see her again." I poured her a glass of water. "You've made a friend in Jim. He's giving Gina a piece of his mind."

I nodded at Jim. He was leaning over Gina with his face inches from her face. We couldn't hear what he was saying but the look on Gina's face was priceless. She had gone pale. Jim let go of her arm and she turned to leave. Jim looked over at us, smiled and gave the thumbs up sign.

I leaned down to her whisper in her ear, "I love you Chelsea. I won't hurt you again. I swear." I kissed her just below her ear. I looked in her eyes and I caught the tear that slipped out with my thumb.

I turned and walked away to meet up with Jim. Jim had been watching me from the doorway.

"What'd you say to her?" he asked.

"I told her I loved her and swore I wouldn't hurt her again. What'd you say to Gina?"

"Same thing basically. I told her you loved Chelsea and that you wouldn't let Gina hurt her. I then told her I'd be watching her to make sure that wouldn't happen."

I thought that must have been when she lost all color. Jim and I walked back to the café and sat down at our table. The signing was almost at an end and Chelsea was wrapping things up. She came over to us at the café. She had a copy of her book in her hand. She handed it to Jim and kissed him on the cheek.

"Thanks for running interference." She said.

"What do I get?" I asked with a pout.

She leaned over me and whispered. "You get your thank you in private."

I smiled and pulled her onto my lap.

"Still say that you don't deserve her." Jim said.

"Whether or not I deserve, I've got her and I'll do my best to keep her."

Chelsea looked surprised. "What's on the agenda for the rest of the day?"

I checked my watch. It was almost three thirty. "I have dinner reservations for six and something for after dinner, but nothing else planned. Was there something you wanted to do between now and dinner?"

"I think I need a nap and then I need to get ready for tonight. What am I wearing?"

"Something dressy, but not too revealing." She laughed, kissed me, and slid off my lap.

"I'm going to catch a cab back to the hotel. I'll be ready at five thirty." She walked away and headed out the door.

I turned to Jim. "I need your help for tonight."

Jim smiled, "Anything. You name it."

"Be at my apartment at around nine thirty. Hang out there until I call. I'll leave directions for you there. I need to pick up a few things for tonight."

"Big plans?" Jim asked.

"Phase one." I smiled and headed out the door to run my errands.

CHAPTER 12

❀

I sat in the cab on the way back to the hotel mentally and physically exhausted. I hadn't counted on Gina showing up at the book signing. It was a little unsettling. She was very unsettling. I was worried that while Payne was still in Philadelphia and I was in New York that she would pull stunts like she did on Friday and today. It was obvious that she didn't want Payne to move on. What was more unsettling was what Payne had done in reaction to Gina.

"I love you Chelsea. I won't hurt you again. I swear."

I was really surprised by that. I was happy with the "I adore you" the night before. I thought I heard him tell me that he loved me last night when he slipped into bed with me, but then I thought I dreamt it. I was skeptical of what he said but at the same time wanted to believe he meant it. I had learned to be cautious a long time ago.

I arrived at the Marriott and headed up to my room. I needed a long shower and a quick nap. It was almost four. I could lie down for about half an hour and then jump in the shower. I was intrigued by what he had planned for the evening. Jim had said last night that he had been looking forward to this all week long. This was such a surprise. I couldn't get used to the new Payne. He actually thought things out more than a day at a time. When we dated in college, he had never been like this.

I was too excited to really sleep. I took about a half an hour shower. After the shower I dried my hair and went to the closet. I had a short black dress for the evening. It had a high neck but was very tight. The back of the dress was very low cut. If I had normal sized breasts I could probably get away without wearing a bra, but since I didn't, I had taken the dress to a seamstress and had a bra built in. I had worn it to Susan's engagement party, much to the unhappiness of my brother. I opted not to wear stockings but instead I wore three-inch heels that were comfortable but looked very uncomfortable. I usually don't wear makeup but decided tonight to go all out. I had lipstick, mascara, and eye makeup. I had put on two layers of Chanel Number Five. I had body lotion on first and then I sprayed the perfume on when I was done. I put my hair up in a twist. I had a purple cashmere wrap to put over my dress.

At five thirty, I went downstairs to the lobby to wait for Payne to arrive. I was very nervous about the evening. Payne walked in a blue suit. His eyes went wide at the sight of me. He walked over to me. With my three-inch heels, he was only about three inches taller than me. He quickly leaned down and kissed me hello.

"You look beautiful." He said. "Are you ready to go?"

"Yes. Dress isn't too revealing?" I put the wrap around my shoulders and we headed out the door. He had his car with him. It was the first time we were driving ourselves somewhere. He had a black Honda Civic. He opened my door for me and I slid into the front seat.

"Where are we off to?" I asked.

"Surprise." He smiled at me. We arrived at the Capital Grille. They had valet parking. I had walked ahead of Payne to the restaurant door while he was getting his claim ticket from the valet. My shawl had slipped and for the first time he saw my dress from behind. The dress clipped behind my neck and then dipped low to the base of my back.

"Chelsea." Payne called. I turned around. "Pick up your shawl." I smiled.

We sat at our table and looked at each other. We had ordered a bottle of wine and were enjoying the appetizers. Payne ordered two different appetizers. The fresh mozzarella wrapped in prosciutto was a Capital Grille specialty while shrimp cocktail was a favorite of mine. It was then that I finally asked after his family.

"How are your parents?" I asked.

"My dad's doing fine. He's still the town sheriff. My mom's not doing as well. She was diagnosed with breast cancer this summer. The treatment has been going well, but we're still really worried. My sister is still in the area. She's married and expecting her first child in January. I go home about once a month to check on my mom. I'll probably head home next weekend to check in with them."

"I'm sorry about your mom. That's tough. I remember when my grandfather was sick. Sometimes the treatment is worse than the disease." I was pushing around the salad. What he had said early in the day was nagging at me. He had told me he loved me. It was kind of hard to believe after all this time apart and so little time together again.

Finally, our main course arrived. I had ordered grilled swordfish steak while Payne had the filet mignon. It was while we were eating our main course that I finally dove into the topic that had been nagging me all day. It had taken most of the bottle of wine before I had enough courage to question him. It took him by surprise.

"Why did you tell me you loved me?" I asked.

"Because I do." He answered very sure of himself. The whole time I knew him he was very sure of himself. Even while he as floundering in school, he was very confident. "We've known each other a long time Chelsea. I know we have been apart for eight years but I can honestly say that I like the way I feel when I am with you. I loved being with you ten years ago and I love being with you now. I've spent a lot of time this past week thinking about the way things were back in college. I noticed that you were such a caring person then. You put up with so much of my shit and I made so many mistakes that you forgave me for. I watched you with Jim and the guys. You were very attentive to me and listened to Jim. I know you think it's quick to tell you that I love you, but I don't know that I ever really stopped loving you. I really want to make this work."

I couldn't help but nod. I couldn't look up at him. I couldn't tell him I loved him. Not right now. I was still afraid. He was very good at reading people and their body language. His next statement made that very clear.

"You don't have to tell me you love me Chelsea. I know you're scared. I know you need to learn to trust me again. I want to prove it to you. Will you let me? That's all I'm really asking for is a chance."

I nodded again. There was a lump in my throat that I couldn't seem to talk through. I continued to eat dinner.

"What are you doing the weekend before Thanksgiving?" He asked.

"I'm in Boston for a signing."

"If I can get my sorry ass up to Boston would you allow me to plan a birthday weekend you will never forget?"

He remembered when my birthday was. That was a good sign.

"I'd love to spend the weekend with you in Boston. I haven't been there in a while." That was the truth. I had gone up to Boston in June with Steve when he moved up there from New York. I was nervous about going up again and this would make it easier.

"Jim has drill that weekend with the guard. He thinks there are orders coming down from above. He is after me to show him the town in New York Thanksgiving weekend."

"Both you and Jim should come out to my parents for Thanksgiving dinner. My dad would love Jim and my brother will think he's a riot."

"I would love a chance to redeem myself in your family's eyes. How hard do you think that will be?"

"I've already spoken to Tommy and Julie about it. My parents will be a harder sell. I'll prepare them. Have you thought about where you're going to live in New York?"

"Actually I found a couple of places; one place in DUMBO and one in Brooklyn Heights. They're about twice what I pay now for half the size but it's close to work." I opened my mouth to remind him about the basement apartment. "Mending fences with your family will be hard enough without living in your basement."

"That's certainly true. If you need to store some of your stuff in my place that's totally fine."

"That I may take you up on."

Payne motioned for the check. "If we don't leave now, we're going to be late."

"Late for what?"

"Second surprise."

We drove to the Annenberg Center. To my surprise, Payne had bought tickets to the opera for the night. What made it even better was the opera being performed was Bizet's *Carmen*. *Carmen* was the first opera I studied in school and the first opera I had seen live. Payne always loved music. He liked almost any type of music. I had been more into popular music that would be played on the radio stations. Payne had loved a variety of music. The one type of music he had no experience with was opera. I, however, had gone to the opera several times with my father and grandfather. I took him to the Metropolitan Opera House in New York City and he began to expand his musical tastes further.

The storyline of *Carmen* was one that was not lost on me. There was interesting parallel between our relationship and the plot. The love of Carmen ruins the young soldier. My love for Payne had almost ruined me eight years ago. I began to have my fears and doubts about the relationships. During the almost hour and a half show, he was very attentive. His arm was often around my shoulder. He would stroke my arms or play with the back of my neck.

After the show was over, we headed back to his apartment. On the way there, he took out his phone and made a call.

"Just me checking in. How's it going? Good. About ten minutes. Thanks. I owe you one."

"What was that about?" I asked.

"Nothing just checking in on a project." He looked over at me and smiled. "Did I tell you what a great time I had tonight?"

"No. Did you?" I smiled.

He picked up my hand and kissed it. We pulled into his parking garage. When he parked in the visitor spot, he explained his situation with his car.

"I usually leave my car at work. It's easier than paying the parking fee at the building. I'm hoping for the same set up in New York. I hear the price of parking a car there is the same as my rent."

"You could always leave it at my house. I have a garage and a full driveway. Not to mention parking on the street."

"I may take you up on that as well. Listen I'm up in New York in two weeks. I want to mend fences with your brother. Do you think I could bribe him with tickets to a NY sporting event?"

"I'll make him go. Although if it is a Knick's game I think he wouldn't care if you were there are not."

"Done deal. I'll check the schedule." We were walking down the hallway on the fourth floor toward his apartment. He opened the door and he let me walk in first.

There was music playing and along the large windows there were candles of various sizes all lit. Spread on the cocktail table in the living room was a bottle of wine with white and red rose petals spread around the table. Payne closed the door and locked it. He walked toward me as the song changed. It was Led Zeppelin's "Hey Hey What Can I Do." He took me in his arms and began to dance with me. He was singing softly in my ear.

I looked up at him and smiled, "Thank you for a wonderful evening." I kissed him quickly and buried my head in his shoulder.

"It's not over yet." He reminded me. We stood together dancing in the candlelight of his apartment. He had programmed a series of songs to play that were reminders of the good times. He had obviously taken the time to go through his rather extensive collection of songs to pull out some of the most memorable in our two years together. Most of the songs were ones that he had introduced me to through his love of classic rock.

As we danced, I was playing with the hair at the nape of his neck. He was stroking the bare skin of my back. He pulled my earlobe into his mouth sending shivers down my spine. He moved his hands down my back and onto my rear end. He slipped his hands inside my dress to find that I had no panties on. He lifted his head from my neck and looked into my eyes completely surprised at the fact he had just discovered. I smiled as he bent his head and kissed me with unbelievable passion. During the kiss, he moved me closer and closer to the living room wall. Before I knew it he had me pinned up against the wall.

As he cupped the back of my neck for another kiss, he unhooked the top of my dress and then reached into my hair and unclipped it. The dress fell forward revealing my bare breasts and my hair fell down around my shoulders. His hands moved down my shoulders and down the black skirt dragging the top of the dress with his hands. My breasts were free of the top of my dress. I thought that he would stop moving his hands down my body at that point and focus on my breasts. I was wrong.

Both hands moved downward. His right hand had moved to his belt buckle and pants. His left hand had worked all the way down to the hem of my dress and was slowly moving back up my thigh taking the dress with his caressing hand. The whole time his hands were moving, his mouth was moving between my mouth and my ear. He was licking my lips and sucking at my earlobes. My skirt was up around my hips when I felt the fabric of his pants fall to the floor. His hands had moved to my bare legs and he picked me up. He pushed me against the wall and thrust into me. I gasped at the depth and the intensity of it. He kept moving quickly breathing into my ear as I tried to move with his urgency. He turned still connected with me and sat on the leather ottoman.

I was straddling him with his face now at the same level as my breasts. I put my feet still in the three-inch heels down on either side of the ottoman and began moving on him. He let me take control of our passion. He buried his face in my breasts pushing them closer together making the licking of both nipples that much easier. The combination of the pressure of Payne inside me and the sucking and stroking of my nipples was pushing me closer and closer to a release. I was worried he had me in such a fever pitch that I would have my orgasm leaving him unfulfilled. What I hadn't noticed was the sweat on his forehead from trying to prevent his own orgasm from arriving too soon. I was beginning to shake with the abandonment of my release.

He looked up at me and I looked into his eyes. He pulled me down to kiss him. As he was about to kiss me, I heard him whisper, "I love you." I put my hands in his hair and kissed him as I gave into my shaking legs and pulsing body as he poured inside me. After the shaking had stopped, I rested my head on his shoulder.

"Wow. I am so glad I didn't know you had nothing on underneath that dress until we got in the apartment. If I had known that you had nothing on, nothing would have gone the way I planned. I'm pretty sure I wouldn't have made it through dinner let alone the opera."

"I'll have to remember that. Even better would be the idea that you will react this way if I decide to not wear underwear in the future."

As much as I didn't want to get up, I was noticing how low the candles were burning. I mentioned that to Payne.

"I'll make you a deal." He said, "you go wait in bed for me, I'll take care of the candles, and then take care of you."

"Sounds like a deal." I said getting up. I stepped out of my dress and saw him watching me walk down the hallway to his bedroom completely naked except for my three inch black sandals.

CHAPTER 13

✾

As she walked down the hallway to my bedroom, I kicked off my pants and took off the rest of my clothes. I moved around the room putting out the candles knowing that she would find more lit in my bedroom and a carpet of rose petals on the bed. I moved to the kitchen and grabbed a bottle of water and a few ice pops out of the freezer.

She was in my bed waiting for me. Jim had done an awesome job setting up my apartment. There were rose petals on the bed and tall white pillar candles on the bedside tables. I approached the bed with the bottle of water in one hand. I stood beside the bed and offered her a water bottle. She took a long drink. I then offered her the desert.

"Otter Pop?" I said smiling.

"What flavor?" She asked.

"Cherry. Is there any other flavor?"

I laughed climbing into bed with her. I ripped off the top one of the ice pops and pushed the ice portion out of the plastic. I put the pop to her lips and watched her tongue trace the edge of the pop. I bent down and kissed the moisture from her lips. I brought the ice pop between her breasts leaving a trail of red juice down her body that I bent to lick from her. She was arching up to meet the licking of my tongue. I moved down between her legs and began to kiss the insides of her thighs. I took what was left of the ice pop and began to tease her with it. The juice of the pop was running between my hands and sliding down her legs. I began to lick at her legs and spread her legs wide. I put the last section of the pop in my mouth and buried my face between her legs. She gasped at the cold of the ice pop and the pressure of my tongue sliding in and out of her. Before the ice pop had melted completely she grabbed my head and pulled me up to suck what was left of it out of my mouth. I took that opportunity to push inside her. She arched up and screamed. I could feel the walls of her vagina tightening around me. I sped up my pace and brought us both over the edge into oblivion.

We were stuck together with sweat and ice pop. We both had red streaks down our bodies.

"You want a quick shower?" I asked. She nodded.

"Who set up the candles and flowers?" She asked getting out of bed.

"I set it up but Jim camped out waiting for the call. He lit the candles and then took off. Go ahead. I'm going to strip the bed. Remember what I said about the shower at the Marriott? Same thing applies here. If I get in, you'll never get out and I'd much rather make love to you in your shower at home.

As she moved into the bathroom and turned on the shower, I pulled the sheets off and replaced them with soft flannel sheets that I hadn't packed yet. I laid out the white silk negligee and card I had bought that afternoon. I went into the bathroom just in time to have her step out and put a towel around her. I grabbed her to my sticky body and kissed her quickly.

"There's something on the bed for you. Give me about five minutes" I jumped into the shower and rinsed off the red juice. I returned to the bedroom to find her in the white silk negligee. The card was unopened in her hands.

"Payne." She began. "I don't know how to react to this weekend. It has been one gigantic roller coaster ride. I'm going to save this card for the ride home tomorrow. I need to digest this one piece at a time."

"Am I trying a little to hard?" I asked moving to the bed.

Nodding her head, she put her thumb and forefinger together meaning just a little. I laughed said, "Ah honey, didn't anyone ever tell you not to make that small sign to a man."

I climbed in bed with her and blew out the candles by the bed. I was happy to sit up in bed with her sitting between my legs. I was sitting up against the headboard.

"Did you make the head and footboard?" She asked as she was stroking my forearms.

"Yes and the dresser as well. I made them the first semester at St. Francis. Contrary to what you think, I wasn't going out as much. My mom and dad were more than a little unhappy with me and my grades at Fairfield."

"Payne," she began hesitantly, "how many women were there while we were together?"

I turned her head around and looked her in the eyes. "There was only Tracey and that was only once. I was really drunk one night and was missing you. Before I knew what was happening it was over. You showed up the next day. It was as if you knew. I was afraid of it happening again. I knew it wasn't fair to either one of us."

"What about after us?" She asked.

"I dated Tracey for about another year until she broke it off. She lives in Pittsburgh and is married with two kids last I heard. I was single for a while. I had a few brief relationships. Nothing meaningful. Gina and I started dating two years ago. At first I thought there was something, but like I said yesterday I've known for the last six months that things were over. I just was too lazy to do anything about it. I needed a reason. New York and you were the reason." I kissed her forehead.

"Chelsea, I know you're scared. I'm scared too. I'm afraid I've hurt you so much you can't forgive me. I'm afraid your family won't accept us. I know how much your family means to you. I could never come between them and you. All I can tell you is that I am willing to try. I want to make it up to you."

She was silent. She was still stroking my arms up and down. I kissed her neck and scooted down in the bed taking her with me. I was leaning over her when I looked into her eyes and probed into her past.

"What about you?" I asked. "Is there someone in New York?"

"No. There's no one in New York." She said.

"Who took my place when I left? I need to know as much as you needed to know about me."

"I didn't get another date on campus at Fairfield. I was still so much in love with you and it seemed everyone knew it. No one wanted to bother. I went on a few dates at home. It was tough because my parents had moved to Hicksville and I didn't know anyone. By the time I started working at Power Memorial, I finally had a few dates with one guy. John and I dated for about six months but something was missing. There was also a friend of Tommy's that I saw for a while. That ended in last June."

"Will you agree to work on this with me?" I asked her.

She nodded.

"Can you please open the card?"

She nodded again.

She opened the card and began to read what I had written.

> Chelsea,
> I want you to know how happy you have made me in the last week and half. I hope that I make you happy and you will let me continue to make you happy.

For the last eight years something in my life has been missing. Sometimes I would stop and wonder where you were and what you were doing. I didn't think I would ever have a chance with you again. I promise to do everything to make you happy and show you how much I love you.
All of my love,
Payne

I watched the range of emotions on her face. She was at first happy at what I was saying to her and then the sadness that I saw puzzled me. I saw the tear slip out of the corner of her eye and her eyes closed.

I caught the tears on my fingertips and turned her head toward to me. "Shh. I didn't want to make you cry again. I only want to see you cry tears of joy."

"They are tears of joy." She explained. "I never thought I would ever get another card from you or another gift. I didn't think I'd ever see you again let alone make love with you again. I've been given such an opportunity that I am crying tears of joy. Do you know I still have all your letters and cards?"

I was surprised at that. It was telling that she didn't throw them out. I couldn't say the same of the things she had given me. I had gotten rid of most of her letters and things after we broke up. Part of me didn't want to be reminded of what I had lost. "Why would you keep all of those things?"

"Why did I get a tattoo of your dagger?"

"Because you love me." I said confidently with a smile. "You don't have to say it. I'll say it for you. You love me, and I love you so much I will wait to hear you say it."

I kissed her and settled her head down on my shoulder and stroked her hair at the nape of her neck. "Let's get some sleep so I can make you an unbelievable breakfast tomorrow. It's going to be hard as hell putting you on a train tomorrow knowing I won't see you for two weeks. And then I'll have to be on my best behavior for older brother."

She fell asleep in my arms and slept quietly through the night. I spent half the night thinking of ways to earn back her trust and prove to her how much I loved her.

CHAPTER 14

I woke up in Payne's bed alone. I heard noise in the kitchen and walked down toward a Payne dressed in sweatpants and a St. Joseph's t-shirt. He was standing over the stove making a cheese and bacon omelet. He heard me come in and turned to me.

"Morning sleeping beauty. This has to be a first. I'm up before you and I actually made breakfast." He said smiling.

I laughed, "You're right. I don't think you ever got up before me. Ever."

"Well breakfast is served. Have a seat." He said motioning to the dining room table. He had set it with two place settings. I went and sat down at one place. He brought over breakfast and put it on the table. He leaned over and kissed me good morning.

"What time is your train?" He asked.

"I was going to try for a two o'clock train."

"Do you want me to take you to the station?"

"That would be nice." I said, "Payne, I don't know how to thank you for everything this weekend. I had a fantastic time."

"There seems to be a but missing." He said with a worried look.

"There is a but. I need time." I said. "I need to time to figure this out. I want to spend time with you, but I also need to do things for myself. I finally have a book published. While you were this unreachable dream, so was this book."

"I understand." He said. "How about setting some ground rules?"

I nodded.

He explained his ground rules. "I'll call you every Wednesday. I already secured four tickets for the Knick's vs. the Suns for a week from this Saturday. I thought maybe I would work on your brother and his wife. The following week I'm moving up to New York and then the following week you're in Boston. I'll come with you to Boston if you still want me to. Jim's coming up for Thanksgiving weekend. We'll see where we are then. OK?"

I nodded amazed that he had thought that far ahead. He had never planned anything before. This was now the third instance of planning since our lives had reconnected.

After breakfast was over, I slipped on the very mussed dress from the night before. I brushed out my hair and put the heels back on. Payne had on a pair of jeans and his St. Joseph's T-shirt.

"You still look beautiful." He said.

I laughed, "I never thought I'd be doing the walk of shame at almost twenty-eight."

We walked out to his car and drove back to the hotel. At the hotel, I hopped in the shower while Payne lay on the bed watching TV. While I was in the shower, I heard the phone ring.

"Phone's ringing." Payne called. "Do you want me to answer it?"

I thought for a minute. "Sure." I hurried to get out of the shower. Payne was still on the phone when I came out of the bathroom.

"No problem. I'll tell her." He said as he hung up.

I was in my blue silk robe with my hair wrapped up in a towel. I put my leg up on the bed and began putting on the Chanel body lotion.

"That's really not fair." He said motioning to my exposed leg. I finished applying the lotion to one leg and put the other one up to do the same.

"Suck it up." She said, "Who was on the phone?"

"Susan." He said watching me pack my bag. "She called to tell me your mom and dad stopped by and want you to come out to the house for dinner on Friday night."

"They stopped by?" I said surprised.

"Yeah. They were on their way home from babysitting the kids last night at Tommy's house."

"Shit." I said. "That means Tommy told them about this weekend."

"Bad?" He asked.

"Could be." I said as I brushed out my wet hair. I took off my robe and began to put on my underwear. Payne wasn't watching the TV anymore but watching me.

"Really Chelsea, you're torturing me." He said.

I laughed, "Get over it. You'll see me again soon enough. Besides that you it's not like you didn't get any this weekend. I haven't had so much sex in one weekend since...." I stopped to think.

"Since we broke up." He said with a smile. "Good to know."

"Shut up." I smiled too. It made me feel like less of a whore. There was something irresistible about Payne.

When I was dressed and ready to go, he was still lying on the bed. I went over to pull him up. I offered him my hand and he pulled me down on top of him.

"Call in sick for Monday." He said pushing the hair away from my face.

"I can't. Everyone at work knows I'm in Philly." I kissed him. "I'll see you a week from Friday. Come on or I'll miss my train and you'll miss the entire football game."

He rolled off the bed and pulled me up. He carried my bag as we made our way down to the lobby. I had express check out so I didn't have to sign any papers. We walked out to his car and made our way to the train station. At the station, he kissed me again and promised to call on Wednesday.

"You'd better." I said and smiled.

"I love you." He said waiting for me to answer. I turned and walked away toward the train. "You love me." He called out to me.

I laughed and smiled, "Do I know you?"

He laughed again and I got on the train. He turned to leave and I was smiling at the memories from the weekend. It seemed like a good start. Things hadn't exactly gone the way I planned. As much as I enjoyed the sex, I hadn't wanted to fall in bed with him. It was hard to go backwards with him. Once you had shared what we shared in college, it was difficult to stop yourself from having that again. I didn't have much to compare the sex with but my other partners had never evoked the same responses from me.

I closed my eyes and fell asleep with the motion of the train

CHAPTER 15

Wednesday came before I knew it. I was excited to talk to Chelsea on the phone. I was busy all week long with the particulars of the transfer. Packing was taking up my time. I had most of my things packed. I had called the apartment buildings in DUMBO and Brooklyn Heights to schedule appointments for the following Saturday to check the places out.

I dialed Chelsea's phone number. She picked up the phone on the second ring.

"Hey beautiful." I said, "What are you up to?"

"I just got out of the shower. I had a great workout at the gym and needed a shower."

"Not fair." I said.

"What's not fair about it?" She asked.

"You just put all sorts of images in my mind." I said. "Are you naked?"

She laughed. "Do you want me to be?"

"Please don't do that! I didn't call to have phone sex. How has your week been?"

"Same as usual. The kids are too funny. They will do the funniest things. Freshmen in particular are so funny. They can be clueless."

"I can't believe you deal with them everyday. I see these kids out on the street and I can't believe them."

"There not so bad. The paperwork stinks. I'm still grading the essay tests I gave last Friday. I'm behind. I spent a little to much time with this guy."

"Anyone I know?" I laughed

"Nah. Hey listen. I'm going out to my parent's house this Friday night. Any ideas?"

"Don't know what to tell you. Just remember that I love you." I said. "I'm heading out to my parents house this weekend. I need to check on my mom."

"Tell her I hope she's doing well. She's such a sweet woman. I don't know how she puts up with you."

"Are you still naked?" I asked.

"You are too much." She laughed. "What a one track mind! No I'm actually in my pajamas getting ready to grade the tests I should have done this weekend. What was your week like?"

"Busy. I'm training the new guy. Packing up my apartment. Which reminds me. I may drive up next weekend. I have an appointment to look at an apartment next Saturday. Could I leave some of my things in your basement?"

"No problem. Did I tell you how impressed my brother was with the tickets to the Knicks?"

"No. So am I still in the basement?"

"Oh babe. Don't get ahead of yourself. You're still outside the house."

I groaned. "Where are we going for dinner before the game?"

"There's a good place a couple of the blocks south of the Garden. Mustang Sally's."

"Sounds good. Listen babe. I better let you go. I don't want to get you in trouble with your students. I'll call you on Sunday after you've been to your parents' house. Are you staying all weekend or just Friday night?"

"I'm not sure. I imagine I'll stay for the weekend. I missed you this week."

"Yeah?" I asked surprised. "I missed you too. The bed's a little too big without you and I can't look in the freezer at those otter pops."

"On that note. Have a good night. I'll talk to you Sunday night?"

"Yes."

"Payne?"

"Yeah."

"One more thing, I'm in bed and naked." She hung up the phone laughing.

I couldn't believe she hung up the phone. She always had a way of being outrageous. If you put her up to a dare, she would do it. There wasn't anything that she could not accomplish. I think that must have been the problem in college. She was succeeding and I was floundering.

On Friday, I headed out to my parents home in Patton, Pennsylvania. My mom had been doing very well with her cancer treatment. She had responded well to the chemotherapy. I made the four-hour drive from Philly to inform them of the good news in my life. They knew I was up for a promotion. I brought a bottle of champagne with me to celebrate the promotion. Even though I was happy, I was worried about being so far from my mom during the treatments.

I pulled into the driveway late on Friday night. I walked in the front door and called out to my parents.

"Mom? Dad?" I called.

"In the kitchen." My mom answered. I walked back to the kitchen to see her stirring soup on the stove. She looked good. She had always been thin but the cancer had made it more pronounced. She lad lost her hair with the first round of chemotherapy and had taken to wearing a wig that was very similar to the way she kept her hair. Her hair had been gray since I was in high school. Instead of making her look older it actually looked better than when she used to dye her hair. I came up behind her and hugged her. She turned and hugged me back.

"What's new?" She said turning back to the soup.

"Turkey bone soup! My favorite." She was in the last stages of it. She was adding the flour dumplings to cook. I put the champagne in front of her. "Are you in the mood to celebrate?"

"What are we celebrating?" She asked.

"I got the promotion. They're transferring me to New York."

"Payne!" She yelled putting down the soupspoon and hugging me. "Bob! She called to my father. Payne's home with news!"

My dad Bob walked into the kitchen. He extended his hand to me. I shook it and he pulled me into a bear hug. He was about the same height as me and had put on little weight over the years. He was about two years from retirement.

"I got the promotion and the transfer." I told him.

"The New York office?"

"Yes. And that's not all."

"I ran into an old friend in New York three weeks ago. Do you remember Chelsea Michaels?"

"The girl you dated at Fairfield?"

"Yes. She teaches in the city and just published a book."

"She was such a nice girl." My mom said. "It was a shame you too didn't stay together."

I smiled because if my mother knew all the things we did together in her own house, she wouldn't think she was such a nice girl. "Well we've been spending some time together lately. If things go well you may not only be a grandmother next year but you may have another wedding."

"Payne." My father said, "that's kind of quick. Are you sure about that?"

"Yes sir." I smiled. "I've got to mend some fences with her and her family but it's what I want."

"Are you working Thanksgiving weekend or are you coming home?"

"I'm working up in New York. Low man works the holiday. Jim Collins is coming up for Thanksgiving. We'll probably go out to Chelsea's for Thanksgiving. I'll be home for Christmas and maybe a weekend in between."

"We'll look forward to seeing you then." My dad said and headed back out to his office.

"How's Jane feeling?" I asked. My sister was in her second trimester of her first pregnancy.

"She's doing fine. Her belly is getting big," my mom laughed. "She's worried about gaining too much weight."

I laughed. My sister had my mother's very slim build. It was difficult for them to gain weight. "Mom, Chelsea sends her love."

"She was always such a nice girl. Of all your girlfriends, I always liked her the best. I'm happy that the two of you have found each other again. I'll pray for you."

"I need all the help I can get." I said sitting down at the table. "How are you feeling?"

"Good today. It depends on the day. One day at a time. So far this seems to be a good day and it's almost over. I took the time to make the soup tonight because the smell wasn't bothering me. It's smells that still get me."

"But the treatments are going well?" I asked concerned

"The doctors are pleased."

"Good. Is Jane coming over tomorrow?" My sister Jane usually came over on Saturday mornings when her husband was sleeping after working the night shift.

"She should be here tomorrow around seven or eight after Kenny gets home from work. Are you hungry?"

"No, I ate on the way. I'm really tired. I think I'm just going to head up to bed."

"Good night then." My mom said giving me a kiss. "It's good to see you Payne."

I hugged her. "It's good to see you too."

I went up to my room and settled in for a decent night sleep. I was excited to see my sister Jane. She had always liked Chelsea and I had hoped to get a woman's pective on what I could do to set things right.

As expected, Jane arrived at seven the next morning. I stumbled into the kitchen to see Jane and my mother sitting at the kitchen table with cups of tea in front of them. Jane got up from the table to greet me when she saw me walk into the room. From what I could see her belly wasn't overly large. It was November and she wasn't due until January. I hugged her and rubbed her little baby bump.

"Mom says you have good news." She said. She looked just like my mom. She was tall and slim like my mom but had brown hair instead of my mother's gray hair. Her face was all smile with the glow that so many pregnant women have.

I went over to the coffee pot and poured a large cup of coffee. "Which good news do you want first?" I asked as I added the cream and sugar.

"There's more than one thing?" she sat back down.

"I got the promotion. I being transferred to New York in two weeks." I said taking a sip of the coffee. I went into the cabinet and grabbed the box of cereal and poured a bowl.

"And…." Jane asked. "What's the other news?"

"I started dated Chelsea Michaels again." I took my bowl and sat down next to Jane. She was initially surprised but smiled.

"When did that happen?"

"I met up with her in New York three weeks ago. Did you know that she has a bestseller?"

"No." Again surprise. "What's the book about?"

"It's a cop thriller. Remarkably the cop is just like me."

Jane laughed. "She was always a riot. Unlike Gina. What's the story with her?"

"It wasn't working out. The move to New York was going to set me free, then I met up with Chelsea and I moved it up a bit."

Jane nodded toward my Mom. She was nodding off at the table. "Mom, why don't you go lie down."

My mom smiled at us and walked out of the room. Jane looked like she was bursting to get information from me. I sat down next to her. Jane was two years younger than I was. While we were younger we fought like any brother and sister would, but in the last few years we had become closer.

"So," she started, "explain the whole Chelsea Michaels thing."

"I ran into her in New York. We had dinner there. She was down in Philly for her book last weekend. We had dinner again and went to the opera. I'm going up next weekend to go to a Knick's game with her brother and sister-in-law."

"This sounds serious." She said sipping her tea.

"It is." I said. "I want to work it out with her. Things ended very badly eight years ago. I have a lot to make up to her. I need to make a plan."

"What do you mean things ended badly? I thought you guys just stopped dating because it was too far between here and Fairfield."

I looked down at my coffee cup.

"Payne," Jane asked, "what happened that you need to make up to her?"

"I cheated on her with Tracey. She arrived here and figured it out. She went back to Fairfield and overdosed on sleeping pills."

Jane was shaking her head. "If you weren't my brother, I'd probably kill you. I don't know how or why she would have anything to do with you after that."

"I can't figure it out either." I admitted. I began eating my cereal again. "I need to convince her that she can trust me. I need to help put the demons to rest. I have a couple of opportunities. I just need a little help."

"What do you have planned?" she asked.

"I bought four tickets to a Knicks game next weekend. We're going to dinner. Her brother Tommy I think would kill me if he had the chance. I need to at the very least sway his opinion of me. She loves her brother. I need to win him over."

"Lay it on the table for him. Tell it like it is. You're always good for that. Explain to him that you can't change things from the past but that you want to make it right. That's your best bet with him."

"That's what I was planning to do. I also have a big weekend planned in Boston for her birthday. What do you think I should do for that?"

"Boston huh?" She said. Jane went to college outside Boston and had inside information about it.

"I want a nice hotel on the water; a good restaurant and something else to do. What do you have for me?"

"Marriott Long Warf for the hotel. Chart House for the restaurant and maybe a carriage ride by the Black Rose at Quincy Market."

I laughed. "I knew I could count on you."

"What are you getting her for her birthday?"

"Definitely jewelry."

"Tiffany's. Every woman should have something from Tiffany's." she said confidently.

"I was going to get her a bunch of presents. I missed so many birthdays. I wasn't such a great boyfriend last time. I want to make up for lost time."

"How many birthdays are we talking about?"

"Eight."

"Tall order. I'll think of some things and e-mail them to you."

"Sounds good."

Jane got up. "How serious are you about Chelsea?"

Without hesitation, "I want to marry her."

"Wow." Jane said. "I'm impressed. She was always good for you. I always liked her. I hope it works out."

"How's mom been lately?"

"Tired but she's responding and doing very well. Don't worry so much. I'll keep you updated." She leaned down to kiss me and I headed up for a shower.

The rest of the weekend was completely uneventful. It was nice being home with my parents and my sister, but something was missing. Chelsea was missing. I found that I couldn't concentrate on anything. I just wanted to see her again, spend more time with her.

CHAPTER 16

I arrived home on Sunday evening from Philadelphia to Susan wanting details. I walked in the door and dropped my bags in the front hallway. Susan came running from upstairs.

"Well," she said, "how was your weekend? As if I didn't know with Payne answering your hotel room phone on Sunday morning."

"Hello to you too." I said. I walked past her into the kitchen. I went to the refrigerator and grabbed a bottle of water.

"Chels, I'm dying!" Susan begged as she sat down on the countertop.

I turned and smiled. "It was great. Really it was." I skipped the run-in with Gina and moved right into Payne showing up at my hotel room with flowers and the night out with his friends. I told her about the book signing and the opera.

"He really went out of his way to make up for time lost. He's different now, more attentive than in college. In college, he wasn't as considerate. I don't know."

"What don't you know?" Susan asked.

"I'm afraid of trusting him completely. I'm afraid it will all fall apart." I said.

"Did you tell him about the overdose?"

"Yeah. He felt like crap. He didn't know about it. I know I'm not the same person. I'm just afraid to become consumed by him again."

"You won't. I know you. You won't."

I walked toward my bags again. I brought them into the kitchen to sort out the dirty clothes. I was pulling out clothes when Susan saw the white negligee.

"New?" She asked picking it up.

"A gift." I said with a smile.

"Really. Flowers and lingerie. So tell me the really important stuff. Is the sex as good as it used to be?"

I turned red.

Susan laughed. "Still that good! What's the next move?"

"He said he'd call on Wednesday. Every Wednesday. This weekend he's going home to see his parents. His mom has breast cancer. It's going well but I can tell he's nervous about it. Next weekend he's coming up to take Tommy and Julie and I to a Knick's game. Sucking up."

"Good move. You need Tommy on your side if you're going to make this work."

"Don't I know that. And you still owe me for that fiasco so you're babysitting next Saturday for Tommy and Julie."

Susan groaned.

"Listen Suz. I want to make this work. I need all the help I can get. He told me he loves me. I want to believe him."

"Do you love him?"

"I must but I'm really afraid."

"Take it slow." She said. "Take it slow."

I started a laundry and called Tommy and Julie. Julie answered the phone.

"Hey Jules."

"How was your weekend?" she asked.

"Great. Listen. Payne's coming up next weekend and he bought four tickets to the Knick's-Suns game on Saturday. Susan has volunteered to baby-sit."

"Tommy should be off that night. I'll ask him. Chels, it really went well?"

"Really. I met his friends, we went out Friday night and then on Saturday we had dinner and went to see *Carmen*. He was really very great. He wants to make it work Jules. Please work on Tommy; you've got to get Tommy to go."

"Knick's tickets is a step in the right direction, but Payne's got to talk to Tommy."

"I know. Are you going out this weekend for dinner?"

"Maybe Saturday. You're on your own for Friday night."

"Thanks for that one." I said less than pleased.

"That was all Tommy honey. He takes that big brother thing very seriously. If you want my opinion, I think he's still mad you broke up with Steve."

"He's got to get over that. Steve and I didn't click."

"Like you and Payne click?" Julie asked.

"As a matter of fact yes. You'll see. Just plan on dinner at Mustang Sally's and the game next Saturday night."

Wednesday arrived and I was more anxious than usual. I was afraid he wouldn't call. I was afraid I was being a fool. I went to the gym to get a good workout in. There was a great weight lifting class I had become addicted to. After the class, I came home and showered. After I had gotten out of the shower, the phone rang. I answered it on the second ring.

"Hey beautiful." He said, "What are you up to?"

"I just got out of the shower. I had a great workout at the gym and needed a shower." Never one to sit still, I had begun to get out my pajamas from my dresser.

"Not fair," he said.

"What's not fair about it?" I asked as I pulled on the pajama pants.

"You just put all sorts of images in my mind." He said. "Are you naked?"

I laughed. "Do you want me to be?" I was actually taking off the robe and putting on my pajama top.

"Please don't do that! I didn't call to have phone sex. How has your week been?"

"Same as usual. The kids are too funny. They will do the funniest things. Freshmen in particular are so funny. They can be clueless."

"I can't believe you deal with them everyday. I see these kids out on the street and I can't believe them."

"There not so bad. The paperwork stinks. I'm still grading the essay tests I gave last Friday. I'm behind. I spent a little to much time with this guy."

"Anyone I know?" He laughed

"Nah. Hey listen. I'm going out to my parent's house this Friday night. Any ideas?"

"Don't know what to tell you. Just remember that I love you." He said. I was kind of flustered and nervous at that. I couldn't say it. "I'm heading out to my parents house this weekend. I need to check on my mom."

"Tell her I hope she's doing well. She's such a sweet woman. I don't know how she puts up with you." I remembered his mom fondly. She was always there when her kids needed her. She made the best turkey soup. I hoped she was doing all right. I knew first hand from watching my grandfather how much cancer could drain a person.

"Are you still naked?" He asked.

"You are too much." I laughed. "What a one track mind! No I'm actually in my pajamas getting ready to grade the tests I should have done last weekend. What was your week like?"

"Busy. I'm training the new guy. Packing up my apartment. Which reminds me. I may drive up next weekend. I have an appointment to look at an apartment next Saturday. Could I leave some of my things in your basement?"

"No problem. Did I tell you how impressed my brother was with the tickets to the Knicks?"

"No. So am I still in the basement?"

"Oh babe. Don't get ahead of yourself. You're still outside the house."

He groaned. "Where are we going for dinner before the game?"

"There's a good place a couple of the blocks south of the Garden. Mustang Sally's."

"Sounds good. Listen babe. I better let you go. I don't want to get you in trouble with your students. I'll call you on Sunday after you've been to your parents' house. Are you staying all weekend or just Friday night?"

"I'm not sure. I imagine I'll stay for the weekend. I missed you this week."

"Yeah?" He asked surprised. "I missed you too. The bed's a little too big without you and I can't look in the freezer at those otter pops."

"On that note." I was embarrassed thinking about it. Sometimes I couldn't believe the situations I found myself in when Payne was around. "Have a good night. I'll talk to you Sunday night?"

"Yes."

"Payne?"

"Yeah."

"One more thing, I'm in bed and naked." I hung up the phone laughing. I loved giving him a hard time. I was smiling as I sat down on my bed and settled into grading the papers that I should have graded instead of spending all my time with Payne. That's one thing I needed to figure out. I was so busy with teaching and my writing that I was afraid I wouldn't have time for Payne.

Friday found me coming home from school and grabbing an overnight bag. What should have been a quick stop became longer as I found a package on my front steps. I opened it to find a bottle of Paddy's Irish Whiskey, my father's favorite drink. The card inside said, "Maybe this will help soften the news that I'm back. Love, Payne" Wow. I couldn't believe he remembered my father's favorite drink. He never really seemed that interested in the details. I guess he was.

I usually took the train out to my parent's house. I kept my car at their house. If I registered it to my house, my insurance rates would no doubt triple. Usually I grabbed the subway and changed at Jamaica to the Long Island Rail Road. The LIRR took me to Hicksville. My dad usually met me at that station and I drove to their house. I was not looking forward to the drive back to the house with my father.

Sure enough my father was waiting with my Jeep at the train station. He had it pulled into the station and was waiting by the front door. It was early November but it was still warm out.

"Hi Daddy." I said and gave him a big hug. "I have something for you." I pulled out the bottle of Paddy's.

"Nice touch, but you still have a lot of explaining to do." He said to me as he gave me the keys. I tossed my bag into the back seat and then hopped into the front seat. My dad got into the passenger side.

"Actually," I said to him as I pulled out into the traffic, "Payne sent the bottle of Paddy's for you."

"Again. There's still a lot of explaining to do. Swing by Raimo's and pick up the pizza. Your mom's working late tonight at the library."

At Raimo's my dad jumped out and picked up the pizza. I was dreading the inquisition I knew was coming. "So do you want to tell me what's going on?" he asked.

"What did Tommy tell you?" I asked.

"He said you spent the weekend in Philadelphia with Payne Williams." He said.

"Kind of. Payne is being transferred with the ATF from Philadelphia to the New York office. I had a book signing in Philly last weekend and we went out to dinner and the opera."

"ATF? Really. I never would have thought he would have gotten it together enough."

"You sound like Tommy. He just had a little too much fun in college. He got his masters at St Joe's in Philly. He's changed dad. Give him a break."

"I'd love to give him a break Chelsea Elizabeth, but he didn't give me much of a break. He wasn't the one who got a phone call at three in the morning telling him his daughter just overdosed on sleeping pills and beer."

We had pulled into the driveway but neither one of us were getting out of the Jeep. The smell of pizza was filling the small wrangler.

"I made those decisions Dad, not Payne. I know you blame him for it, but you should blame me." I paused. "Do you believe in me?"

"Of course I believe in you. What kind of question is that?"

"It's a logical one. You, Tommy, Julie, and I guess mom, are all worried about me getting hurt again. I won't lie I am too, but I worry about getting hurt with any guy. But you all seem to think I'm still nineteen and will make a stupid mistake like taking a bunch of sleeping pills with beer. You need to trust me. You need to believe in me and my ability to make a good decision. Have I made a really bad decision lately?"

"No," he said. My father began to think. "I never really saw it that way. All I could see was the pain that followed when Payne left. I blamed him for it. I just want you to be happy."

"He's making me happy dad. Really he is." I opened my door. "He has to work Thanksgiving weekend and I'd love to invite him to dinner. One of his friends will be in town and I'd love for them to come to dinner."

"You know they would be welcome for dinner." My dad was walking into the house with the pizza. "He's got to earn my trust again Chelsea. I trust you. I just don't trust him."

"Fair enough. All I'm asking for is a non-hostile environment."

"Fair enough."

Julie, Tommy, and the kids arrived at my parent's house on Saturday. We had a good time. Tommy and my father had their heads together at one point. Tommy conceded to giving me a chance with Payne. He, like my father, wasn't ready to give Payne a clean slate. The Knick's tickets were just one step in the right direction.

By the time I left Sunday evening, I was feeling good about Payne's chances with my family. I know they let go of my depression years ago but because it was associated with my break up with Payne it became an issue again. I had hoped I made the point of separating the two.

The phone call from Payne came as promised on Sunday.

"Hey babe." I said. "How was your weekend?"

"Good and from the tone of your voice, I take it yours went well?" he asked.

"The Paddy's was a hit. Thank you for that. Completely unnecessary. You and Jim are both welcome for Thanksgiving dinner."

"That's good to know." He said.

"How's your mom?" I asked. "I know how hard the treatment can be."

"She's holding her own. She sends her love. She's praying for us. She said you were the favorite of all my girlfriends."

"Really?" I said nervously, "And how many girlfriends have your parents met?"

"Chelsea. You're only one of four girls my parents ever met; Mary, my high school girlfriend, you, Tracey and Gina."

"Sorry." I said, "I'm trying Payne. I know I have to let go. What's pretty amazing is I spent most of the weekend trying to convince my family to do the same thing."

"I know being apart is what makes you nervous. It's not for much longer. Before you know it I'll be in New York full time. Listen. I'll be up Friday night around eight or nine. You decide what you want to do."

"OK. I'm sorry Payne. I'm really trying."

"I know babe. I know. I love you. Call you Wednesday?" he asked.

"Not unless I call you first." I said.

"That's my girl." He said.

CHAPTER 17

I drove up to New York from Philadelphia in Friday night traffic that can make the simplest trip nerve racking. Things were looking up for me. On Wednesday, Chelsea actually called me. I was pleasantly surprised and very thankful that she had taken the initiative. It made me feel as if I she had begun to forget all the things I had done wrong the last time we dated. One of the major mistakes I had made was not calling. I had hoped by telling her every Wednesday, it would give her some comfort. I had shown that I could be reliable.

I arrived at her house in Astoria at around eight-thirty. I pulled in the driveway and parked in the back by the garage. I was getting out of the car when she came out the back door. She had on jeans and tight black turtle neck sweater. In her hand was a Carlsberg. She walked down the back porch steps to the car.

"How was the drive?" She asked putting the beer on the hood of the car and her arms around my neck.

"Long." I pulled her into me and gave her a kiss. "I missed you."

"I missed you too." She said. "Are Susan and Joe still standing in the dining room watching?"

I looked over her shoulder and saw them looking out the window. I waved. "Yes. Is this round one of winning over your family?"

"This is the pre-game show. The main event is tomorrow night." She grabbed the beer as I reached into the back seat for my bag.

"It's OK that I stay here tonight? Susan's not going to have a problem with it?" I asked.

"It's my house technically, but no I think she's half in your camp."

I walked in the back door to find Susan and Joe in the kitchen. Susan was making popcorn in the microwave.

"Hey Payne." Susan said. "This is my fiancé Joe."

I shook Joe's hand as he asked, "You're with ATF right?"

"Yeah." I said. He was wearing a NYPD shirt but so did a lot of people after September eleventh. "Are you NYPD?"

"Yeah I used to be on the trains, but now I'm at One Police Plaza."

"I'm moving up next weekend from Philadelphia. I have a couple of appointments tomorrow starting at ten to check out apartments."

"Where?"

"DUMBO and Brooklyn Heights."

"DUMBO's steep. You should just rent the apartment downstairs."

"I offered it, but Payne needs to get on my parents' good side and somehow moving in here wouldn't be a step in the right direction."

"What are you guys up to tonight?" Susan asked as the popcorn finished. She took the bag out of the microwave and found a big white Pyrex bowl to put it in.

"What do you want to do?" Chelsea asked me. The popcorn smelled good and I really just wanted to stay in. It had been a long week of training and packing.

"Can we stay in tonight? I've got that early appointment tomorrow and I'm beat from battling the turnpike."

"Whatever you want. Did you get any good movies Suz?"

"There are bunch in the living room. A few action movies for the boys." Susan replied as she grabbed the popcorn. "Geez Payne, you must be getting old. You turned down going out. Grab some beer from the fridge"

I laughed and grabbed two more beers from the fridge. "There's something to be said with staying at home and watching some testosterone movies." Joe held his beer up to toast me.

We all moved into the living room. We settled in to watch the movie. Joe and Susan sat on the couch together while I grabbed one of the two chairs that faced the TV. I pulled the footstool that went with the chair over and motioned for Chelsea to join me in the chair. She sat between my legs and leaned back. I kissed her neck asked her if she wanted a back rub. She nodded her head. I began to rub her back and neck in a casual way. Pretty soon I was working out knots in her back that apparently had been there awhile. I remember the film being something of an action movie. My mind was more on Chelsea. She became more and more limp as I was massaging her shoulders and back. Before I knew it she was actually asleep. I swung her legs up over the arm of the chair and put her head on my shoulder. I continued to watch the movie and brush the hair away from her face and neck. I could see Susan glance at me every once in a while to check on Chelsea and I. I think she was happy at what she saw.

When the movie ended, Susan got off the couch and stretched. She looked over at me. I wasn't in the most comfortable position. Chelsea was cradled in my lap and I was stroking her arms and her hair.

"She hasn't been sleeping much." Susan explained. "She's very nervous about this weekend."

"I figured as much. I want you to know Suz, I never meant to hurt her in college. I broke it off with her to avoid hurting her and it blew up in my face. I'm here to stay this time. I know I have a lot to make up for and a lot of people to convince that I'm serious about her." I looked down at her when I said this. She was sleeping peacefully.

"She's nervous about loving you again. I know she loves you Payne, but she won't admit it. Keep working on her. We're gonna scoot back to Joe's apartment."

"OK. Will I see you guys tomorrow?"

"Probably not. We have baby-sitting duty. Penance for ratting you out to Tommy."

"I was going to feel sorry for you but now I don't." I shook Joe's hand from where I sat with Chelsea on my lap. "Thanks for everything Suz."

"For what?"

"For taking care of her, for being on my side." I said.

"Make it right Payne. Just make it right." She said.

"I'm working on it." I said.

When the front door closed, Chelsea woke up. She looked at me and smiled. "How long have I been asleep?"

"About a hour." I kissed her and she wiggled on my lap to deepen the kiss.

"I missed you." She said when she broke away and began kissing my neck.

"How much?" I asked. She had begun to move her hands to my shirt buttons.

"Why don't we go upstairs and I'll show you?"

"Sounds like a plan."

She stood up and stretched. When she stretched her sweater rode up and revealed her flat stomach. I reached out to her as I stood out of the chair. She shook her head and pulled her black turtleneck over her head. She turned toward the stairs and crooked her finger at me. I happily followed her. At the stairs she took off her bra and tossed it to me. She turned before I could even catch a glimpse of her naked breasts. She walked up the stairs leaving me staring at her bare back. After a pause, I ran up the flight of stairs to hear the water in the tub being turned on.

I opened the bathroom door to find her bent over the tub. She had taken off her jeans and was wearing a black lace thong. She was lighting candles on the windowsill and filling the tub with bubbles. I turned the lights off in the bathroom and moved up behind her. She had just straightened from swirling the water in the tub. I put my arm around her waist and pulled her back to my front. I began to kiss the side of her neck. I moved up to her ear and began to suck on the lobe. Her knees began to give and her breathing became heavy. She quickly turned around and began pulling at my shirt. I in turn pushed her thong down. She stepped away from me long enough to step out of them and then climbed into the half full tub.

I quickly took off my pants and shirt and jumped into the tub. The water was hot and the bubble bath she had put into the tub was growing. The tub had looked bigger than it was and there wasn't as much space between us.

"I should have ordered the next size up." She said as she straddled me. The water was running behind her and with the two of us in the tub it was dangerously near the top. The bubbles were all over the place. "And maybe I put too much bubble bath in."

I put my bubble-covered finger to her lips to quiet her. I reached up with my foot to turn off the water. "It's perfect. You're perfect."

I kissed her on the lips and grabbed her hips and slowly pushed inside her. Her mouth opened in a gasp and she arched into my chest. The bubbles against her back made her slick and her skin even smoother. She began to move herself on me as I kissed her lips. The water began to slosh out of the tub and onto the platform that had been built on the floor. As she moved more and more rapidly, I began to rub the bubbles into her breasts. She arched back again and moaned. I slid my hands down the sides of her body and grabbed her hips. I took over the movement of her hips. She was beyond reason at this point. I began to feel her tighten around me and took one hand from her hip to grab her neck. I pulled her mouth to mine and thrust my tongue inside her mouth. She grabbed my head in her hands and screamed into my mouth as her body began to shudder around me. The squeezing of her contractions was too much for me and I orgasmed. She collapsed on me.

"I think my leg is asleep." She said into my neck. I laughed and stroked her back.

"Was it worth it?" I asked.

"Without a doubt." She said.

I let the water out of the tub and eased out of her. She groaned. She always hated the feeling of me leaving her body. She clenched to try to keep me inside her. "Come on. Lets get to bed." She finally stood up in the tub. I was still seated and I moved my hands up her legs. She jumped and quickly got out of the tub. She grabbed a towel and wrapped it around her. She offered me a towel and I followed her out of the tub. She threw a few more on the water on the floor and headed into the bedroom.

I was standing in the doorway with my towel wrapped around my waist when she dropped hers and climbed into her bed. I just stood there for a moment. The candles had burned themselves out in the bathroom and the moonlight was coming through the window next to bed.

"Are you coming to bed?" She asked.

I walked over, dropped my towel, and got into bed.

"Thanks for christening the tub with me." Chelsea said, "I've always wanted to have sex in my Jacuzzi tub. I remember thinking about it when they installed the tub. I had thought it was big enough for two but it was a tight fit."

I smiled and pushed her hair away from her face, "Tight fits are always the best."

She laughed, "I missed you. You always did have the best sense of humor. You always could make me laugh."

"I'm glad I could break in the tub with you. I always love when we have a first."

"You're connected to a lot of the firsts in my life; most of them really great. What time are your appointments tomorrow?"

"They start at ten. I guess that means we should get some sleep. I don't want you too tired for the game tomorrow night. That wouldn't be a way to endear myself to your brother."

"Why; do you think he would put two and two together?"

"More like one and one and a bed. He would think I only want your body." I said stroking her shoulders and arms.

"Do you?" she sounded uncertain.

"I love you. All of you. I love your body, your mind, your heart, your soul." I kissed her and pulled her to me. "I love you so much I'll give up this one night of sex with you for all the nights that we will have together. I want forever and if letting you sleep tonight will get me closer to forever, I'll do it."

A tear slipped from her eyes as she closed them. I pulled her to me and put her head down on my chest. I could feel the tears on my bare chest. I began rubbing the hair at the base of her neck. This almost always put her to sleep.

"Shh." I whispered. "Everything will be OK. I promise."

CHAPTER 18

❀

I woke up and Payne was still asleep. It was only eight. I got up and grabbed my robe. I needed a shower to wake up. I had trouble sleeping all week. I was anxious about the game tonight. I was worried something would go wrong. I finally slept hard last night. I remembered crying softly as I lay on his chest. He stroked the nape of my neck until I fell asleep. Now still sleeping in my bed, I kept remembering his words.

"I want forever and if letting you sleep tonight will get me closer to forever, I'll do it."

"I want forever." I couldn't believe he had said that. Did I want forever? Of course I wanted forever. I wanted forever so badly it scared me. I was crying tears of fear and tears of joy last night. To have him say that to me last night had been a dream come true.

I turned on the shower and stepped into the water. I was so lost in my thoughts as the water was coming down that I didn't hear the door to the bathroom open and Payne open the shower door.

"Hey babe." He said as he stepped into the shower. "What time is it?"

"A little after eight. Will you scrub my back?" I said turning around.

"Gladly. Your front gets me into too much trouble." He said. "How much time do we have?"

"Not enough for what you're thinking." I said. "Where are your appointments?"

"I have two appointments. One at Courthouse Street and one at Sixty-fifth Street. Both in Brooklyn."

"We need to get moving." I turned around and gave him a kiss. I stepped out of the shower and put on my robe. I quickly grabbed a pair of jeans and shirt. I was dressed and ready to go when he came into the bedroom.

"Crap that was fast." He said, "I didn't even get a chance to see you get dressed. Little things get me through the day."

I lifted up my blue shirt and flashed him my navy blue lace bra. "Good enough?"

He laughed, "That'll do for now. Is my bag still downstairs in the kitchen?"

"Should be." I said moving toward the stairs. He followed me with the towel still wrapped around his waist. In the kitchen, he grabbed boxers out of his bag and pulled them on. He was bent over the bag getting out his jeans when I smacked him on his ass.

"Hey." He said, "What was that for?"

I smiled grabbing my purse, "Little things get me through the day. Are you ready yet? You're worse than a woman."

"No, I'm not. We're just not all morning people." He said pulling out his toothbrush. "Just have to brush the pearly whites."

"First appointment is where?" I asked. He came out of the bathroom.

"Court Street. It's a smaller place than the one in DUMBO, but less expensive. If it's available I'll take it. It's not that far from work."

"There's really no direct subway route from here. That's what sucks. We can grab the N and transfer to an R train. That will take us there but we'll have to ride all the way through Manhattan. Come on we need to move."

We stopped at Dunkin Donuts and grabbed coffee and egg sandwiches for breakfast.

"When are you moving yourself up?" I asked once we settled on the N train.

"I have a U-haul reserved for next weekend. Jim and the guys will help load me up in Philly. Do you have any good kids I could bribe to get me unloaded?"

"I think I could find you a few that need some community service hours for school."

"I've got a room at the Marriott Long Wharf in Boston for your birthday."

"You're crazy. I would never have booked that. There's another one a little further away that doesn't have the views and is less expensive."

"Government rates. Remember."

"Any other plans for the weekend?"

"For me to know and you to find out."

We switched to the R in Manhattan and surprisingly were ahead of schedule. At Court Street, the building was easy to find. We met with the superintendent of the building. He gave Payne and I the tour. It was a studio apartment with an alcove that could be used as a bedroom. There was a balcony off the living room that had a view of the downtown Manhattan skyline.

"When is this available?" he asked.

"Today if you want." The super answered.

He looked at me. "What do you think?"

"It's nice. We can get a screen for between the alcove and the living room." I answered.

"I'll take it. I'll be up next weekend with furniture." He shook the super's hand and smiled at me. "One down. Two to go."

"Two to go?"

"Tommy and Julie."

I laughed at his list. He paid the security, cancelled his next appointment, and we hopped the three train back into Manhattan. I showed him the direct route to my school from his apartment. At school, I left a note for the Key Club advisor Father Degnan. He would find me a few able bodied young men to haul boxes for Payne the next weekend. By the time we headed back to Astoria it was almost two.

"What time is dinner?" Payne asked.

"We need to be at Mustang Sally's by five for a good table. The game starts at seven."

I helped Payne unload the contents of his car into the basement apartment. I commented on the size of the apartment he was renting.

"I only signed a one year lease, Chels."

"But still $2000 a month for a studio. That's more than my mortgage."

"We all can't inherit a prime piece of real estate." He joked.

"True. Some of us have to remain spoiled brats to give the rest of you something to strive for."

"Are you changing before we head out to the game?" Payne asked.

I checked my watch. It was almost three thirty. "I don't think so. There's not a whole lot of time."

"Oh well. Can't blame me for trying." He smiled down at me. "We don't have time for a quickie do we?"

"There's no such thing as a quickie with you and I. You should know that from the weekend at your parent's lake house."

He laughed remembering how his mother had almost walked in on us in a very compromising position. He leaned me up against the wall anyway and began kissing my neck.

"Could I convince you otherwise?" he asked pushing his hips into mine. He was fully aroused.

"Maybe." I said rubbing back with my hips. I moved my hands around to the waist of his pants. I slipped my hands inside to grab his ass and push him further into my hips. "What do I get later?"

"I'll think of something not as quick." He said moving his mouth down the side of my neck. My hands were busy getting his pants off while he was stripping off my jeans. Before I knew where I was going, I was laying on the floor of the basement apartment my jeans were on the other side of the room and we were having our quickie.

When all was said and done, it wasn't even three forty-five. I had just enough time to get my appearance back together before we left for the game. I was more than a little nervous and Payne could read that. On the subway ride he held my hand and squeezed it a few times when I would get lost in thought.

Mustang Sally's is a few blocks south of Madison Square Garden and on game nights enjoys a brisk crowd. We were early and got drinks at the bar by the door. I needed to get at least one drink in me to relax. I was worried it would turn into a disastrous event. Julie and Tommy walked in the door at ten to five. I waved to them.

"Here goes." I said to Payne taking the last drink out of my pint.

"Just remember something." He said looking down at me.

"What?" I asked nervously.

"I love you."

I smiled and turned to face my brother and Julie.

CHAPTER 19

❧

I hadn't remembered Tommy being so big. If anything, he had put on more muscle in the eight years since I had seen him. He was easily six foot five and at least two hundred twenty-five pounds. He had the same auburn hair as Chelsea but brown eyes. Julie was tiny in comparison. She was shorter than Chelsea. I remembered meeting her once while we were dating.

We went to our table, a booth in the back of the restaurant. Julie and Tommy sat on one side while we sat on the other. I was happy it was a booth. Chelsea needed all the encouragement possible. I could easily show her my support under the table with us sitting next to each other on the same bench.

"Did you get your apartment?" Julie asked. She had a diet coke in front of her while the rest of us had pints of beer.

"On Court Street in Brooklyn Heights. It wasn't as expensive as the ones in DUMBO."

"Better bet. That won't be as long a ride to work as well." She commented. Tommy seemed to be brooding. He hadn't said anything past hello. Chelsea was halfway through her second beer she was so nervous and poor Julie was carrying the conversation with small talk. I decided to lay it all out on the table.

"Listen," I said. "From what Susan told me last night, Chelsea hasn't slept all week worrying about tonight. I know there's a lot of baggage that comes with me walking back into her life. We're working those things out. All I'm asking for is a chance. For her sake not for mine. I love her, you mean the world to her, and that means I need your approval. I don't have to be your best friend. I just don't want her going through another week like this not sleeping because she's worried you'll kill me. Can we just try to start over?"

Chelsea kicked me under the table. Julie's mouth dropped and Tommy laughed a sincere laugh.

"Shit. That had to be the most direct cut to the chase opening ever." Tommy laughed again. "I forgot how direct you could be."

I smiled. "I aim to please."

"The one person you need to please is her." Tommy said pointing at Chelsea. "As long as we're getting it out in the open. If you fuck around on her again, it won't matter you're a federal agent, I'll cut your dick off, stick up your ass, and then I'll kill you."

"Tommy!" Chelsea said and it was my turn to laugh.

I put my hand out to shake his. "Since I'm not going to screw up this time, it won't matter but you've got yourself a deal."

We shook hands and Tommy finally loosened up a bit. I put my hand down next to Chelsea's leg and gave her knee a squeeze. It was going to be all right. The rest of the night was relatively uneventful. The game was decent. Tommy and I sat next to each other and talked sports throughout the game.

At halftime, Tommy and I headed up to the bathroom. Chelsea had a worried look in her eyes. Tommy caught it. "Don't worry. I won't kill him in the bathroom."

We were on line when Tommy asked me a question I didn't expect, "Did she tell you about Steve?"

"Steve?" I asked.

Tommy whistled. "He's the last guy she dated. He actually lived in the basement apartment of her house. He was a friend of mine from Fordham that was doing his residency in Manhattan. I thought he would be good for her, but it didn't work out the way I planned."

I was shocked. I had no idea there had been someone that serious. We made our way back to our seats for the second half. I kept looking over at Chelsea but she wouldn't look at me. It was as if she knew what Tommy had told me. I took her hand and she finally looked at me. "It's OK." I said. She nodded and went back to talking to Julie about Susan's upcoming wedding.

"The Eagles are playing the Giants in two weeks." Tommy said. "Who do you think will win?"

"The Eagles," I said without a pause. "Chelsea and I are in Boston that weekend."

"You're missing the Eagles game to go to Boston with her? You are desperate to get her back." Tommy asked.

"She has a signing and I told her I would plan something special for her birthday while she was in town. I booked a room at the Marriott Long Wharf."

Chelsea turned to us and made a comment, "I didn't think it was possible, but I think Jim is bigger than Tommy."

"Who's Jim?" Tommy asked me.

"Jim Collins works at ATF with me in Philly. He's coming up Thanksgiving weekend to see New York. He's a captain with the Pennsylvania Army National Guard. He's convinced he's about to be deployed."

"Really? That sucks." Tommy said, "I think Julie said you guys are coming out to my parents for Thanksgiving. My dad will love that. He was in the Naval reserve until a few years ago. You should go out on Wednesday night. It's the best night to go out. Chelsea, you should take them to see Sean at Jackie Reilly's."

When the game ended, we walked down to Penn Station. We rode the train to 14th Street with them and then went our separate ways. Tommy shook my hand and I gave Julie a kiss on her cheek.

"Make her happy." Julie said to me.

"That was my plan." I said with a smile.

It was late and we actually got a seat on the train. I pulled Chelsea onto my lap. She was playing absently with the hair at he back of my neck when I asked her about Steve.

"Were you going to tell me about Steve?" I asked quietly. She stopped playing with my hair.

"Eventually." She answered. "I imagine Tommy told you about him."

"He mentioned him." I countered. "So?"

"I'd rather not go into it tonight. I've been trying to come up with a way to thank you since dinner."

"Thank me? For what." I asked.

"For telling Tommy you loved me."

"Chelsea," I picked her head up off my shoulder and made her look in my eyes. "I do love you. I'm not afraid to admit it to him or anyone else. I'll tell your parents on Thanksgiving if you want, but you need to believe me. I don't care if anyone else believes me but you."

She nodded and put her head back down. Before we knew it we were walking back to her house from the train. "I think I have a way for you to thank me." I said to her.

"Yeah?" she asked intrigued.

"Just go upstairs when we get home and hop in bed. Leave the rest up to me."

Her eyebrow was up as she unlocked the door. "I'm giving you five minutes." She said climbing the stairs to her room. I headed back into the kitchen. I remembered seeing fresh strawberries and whipped cream in the refrigerator last night when I had gotten the beer for the movie. I grabbed a bowl from the closet and I put a few strawberries in a bowl and poured the whipped cream on top.

Chelsea was in her underwear when I walked into the room with the bowl in my hand. She looked at it and looked at me. She walked over to me in the doorway. "Is that desert?" she asked putting her finger in the whipped cream and then putting it in her mouth.

"We'll see." I said putting my finger in the whipped cream and putting it to her mouth. She took my finger in her mouth as she reached behind her and unclasped her bra. "Can I put this down by the bed?"

She took the bowl out of my hand and walked over to the bed. She turned down the covers and sat on the bed. She took a strawberry out of the bowl while I started pulling off my clothes. She bit the end off and was looking at me when I leaned down to take the rest of the berry out of her hand.

I got in bed and pulled her down next me. I lay on top of her and picked up another berry. I made sure it had whipped cream on the tip. I went to put it in her mouth but at the last minute moved it down her chin and throat and back up again leaving a line of whipped cream. I let her bite at the berry while I licked up the whipped cream. I grabbed a handful of whipped cream and began to trace a line from the hallow in her throat to between her breasts. She arched up as I began the process of licking up the cream again.

"Payne." She whispered as I took another strawberry covered in whipped cream out of the bowl. I drew the line again further down her flat belly to her belly button. I put the berry in her belly button and began to trace the line of cream down her stomach until I reached the berry again. I picked it up in my teeth and brought it up to her mouth. She bit at as she kissed and licked my lips.

While she was licking at my lips I had begun to massage her breasts. I was caressing her right breast with my left hand while the right one moved between her legs. She pushed her hips upward against me as I inserted my finger inside her. She was slick with moisture and beginning to moan in the back of her throat. By the time she was reaching her climax she had no idea what I was doing.

I pushed her breasts together and knelt above her moving my penis in between her breasts. I thrust about three or four times before I came all over her chest. She was genuinely surprised by what had just happened.

I settled in bed beside her remembering her reaction to my semen on her belly. I began rubbing the semen into her chest and watched her close her eyes in pleasure once again.

"Thank you," she said smiling.

"Your welcome." I said pulling her back against my front falling asleep.

CHAPTER 20

❦

I woke up Sunday morning itchy from the dried whipped cream. Payne was already awake and staring at me. I smiled reaching up to stroke his cheek. It was around nine.

"Do you still go to mass on Sunday?" I asked.

"When I'm home with my parents, yes. When it's just me, it depends."

Nothing had changed in that department. When Sunday came, you could almost always find me at church. My parents had sent me to Catholic School my entire life and certain things stuck with me. Going to church was one of them; the idea of no pre-marital sex and no birth control obviously weren't things that stayed with me.

"I'd rather stay here, shower and have you explain Steve to me." He said.

"I'd rather shower and go to Church." I said. I tried to get out of bed and he rolled over on top of me.

"I'd rather talk about Steve." He said staring into my eyes.

"I'm really not ready for this discussion Payne." I said. "Please."

He looked hurt but nodded. "Shower and Church it is." He got up and went into the bathroom. I heard the water turn on. I had pushed him too far. I don't know what was so difficult to tell him about Steve. I needed to get past it. I decided to get it over with.

I walked into the bathroom and opened the shower door. I stood in front of him and looked up. The water off his back was splashing me in my face. I couldn't continue to look him in the face. That would make it easier.

"Steve moved in here about two years ago. He moved into the basement apartment. He was doing his residency at NYU. It was convenient for him. He was living here a year when I came home really drunk. Before I knew it, we had sex. He wanted so much more from me than I was willing to offer. It was convenient for me. He lived downstairs and when I was lonely, I would go down and hang out with him. He moved out about six months ago when I wouldn't marry him."

He pushed me up against the glass of the shower wall and seriously put his face close to mine. "What did you say?"

"He wanted to marry me. He had a ring and everything. I couldn't do it."

"Why?" he said staring into my eyes.

"It wasn't right. I didn't love him the way he loved me. I'm afraid I won't ever love someone enough to marry them." I looked down.

He tilted my head up and looked me in the eyes. "You will. I promise you. Come on. Let's get to church before we get struck by lightning."

I felt a huge relief wash over me. I hadn't told him Steve moved to Boston but at least I told him about the proposal. Maybe Tommy did me a favor.

After Church, Payne left for Philadelphia. It wasn't so hard to see him leave because I knew he would be back on Saturday. Well not back at my place but at least in New York. I watched him pull out of the driveway and began to wonder what he thought of the Steve situation.

I was able to line up four juniors who needed community service hours. Saturday, I met them at the school and we took the Number Three down to Court Street. We were hanging outside the building when Payne arrived with the U-Haul truck. Jim had agreed to drive his car up to New York Thanksgiving weekend. He could live without the car for the week and a half. He pulled the U-Haul in front of the building and we began unloading his boxes. The boys unloaded the boxes to the curb and then began taking the heavy furniture up to the fifth floor apartment. Moving in New York City was a wonder of the modern world. The furniture was the hardest part. After the furniture was moved up. The boxes were easy. As soon as all the boxes but one load were upstairs, Payne left to return the U-Haul truck, while I went upstairs to the apartment. I ordered pizza and soda for the boys. Typical guys they had unpacked the TV and all the electronic equipment. They had finished setting it up when the pizza arrived.

"Miss M. Who's this guy we're helping out? Your boyfriend?"

The guys all stopped eating and waited for me to answer. I looked over at them from the kitchen area. I was busy washing and putting away all the dishes. I didn't see Payne walking in the door.

"You could say that."

"Say what?" Payne asked.

I jumped as he walked into the kitchen. The boys were quickly absorbed in their pizza. "That you're my boyfriend."

He smiled at me. "Teacher's got a boyfriend." He bent his head and kissed my cheek whispering "Thanks hon. For everything."

He went and joined the boys in the living room. I continued to unpack the dishes. He sat on the red leather couch and called to me in the kitchen. "Can you come in here and help me figure out where to put everything? The boys need to get going and they need a woman's direction."

I walked into the living room. They had set up the entertainment center against the only full wall, but the couch and chair had yet to placed. The small alcove off the living room had his mattress up against the wall with the frame and headboard needed construction. All the boxes were piled in there to stay out of the way.

"I'd say to put the couch facing the entertainment center making a division between the alcove and the living room. Your desk should go in the corner by the balcony. Put the table by the kitchen island. The bed goes up against the window with the dresser in the corner closest to the closet."

They all looked at me in wonder. I turned to go back to the kitchen. I turned at the kitchen door and said, "Well, what are you waiting for?"

"Wow. OK boys, let's get going." Payne got up from the couch and they began moving the furniture to their new places. When they were done, they called me over to have me inspect their handy work. I gave my approval and Payne walked the boys to the elevator.

"Nice boys." He said standing in the kitchen door. "I gave them each $20."

"Payne," I said, "they were here for community service hours!"

"They earned their hours." He said moving toward me. "Now how am I going to pay you?"

I smiled at him and came forward. I leaned into him and whispered against his lips, "You can't afford me." I walked past him. The kitchen was officially done and I moved into the alcove where all the other boxes were located.

"You are so fresh." He said. I had taken off my sweatshirt to reveal a tight tank top. "And so very distracting."

"Are you going to help me unpack or what?" I said looking up at him. I was sitting on the floor on the alcove surrounded by boxes.

"Is there a particular box you are looking for?" He asked.

"I usually make the bed first and then unpack from there."

He looked around and found a box in the corner. He ripped open the top and pulled out the bedding. "Now what do I get?"

I walked over to him and pulled the bedding. He came with the bedding. "Help make the bed and then you can pay me back."

He moved with lightning speed and began to help me make the bed. When we were finished he pulled me down onto the bed. He rolled me onto my back and began kissing me. He leaned up on his elbows and looked into my eyes.

"Did I tell you today how much I love you?"

I shook my head.

"Did I tell you today how much I missed you?"

I shook my head again.

He began kissing my neck and whispering in my ear. "What do you want?"

"You." I gasped. I began moving restlessly against him.

"Your boyfriend?"

"My boyfriend." I said.

CHAPTER 21

❦

I was nervous about the weekend in Boston. I didn't want to overwhelm her. She had finally called me her boyfriend and in front of students no less. To me it was a gigantic step. It seemed that we were moving in the right direction, but I didn't want to end up going backwards. Chelsea offered to go out to her parents' house and retrieve her car for the weekend in Boston. She rode the train out after work on Thursday and drove back late Thursday night. The plan was for me to meet her at the house on Friday afternoon from work.

When I walked into the house Friday, she had her jeep packed and ready to go. It was around five when we left. With traffic, it would take us around four to five hours to drive up to Boston. The hotel had parking that came with the room so there was no worry about the soft-top Jeep. I watched her in amazement on the ride up. I had never really pictured her in a Jeep.

I was smiling at her. "What's so funny?" she asked.

"I was wondering what made you buy a Jeep."

"Have you ever seen *Revenge*?" She asked. I shook my head. "It's one of Kevin Costner's early films. He has a Jeep and goes off to a mountain cabin with Madeline Stowe. They end up having a little fun while he's driving his jeep."

"I might have to see that."

"Why see it when you could live it?" She said with a laugh.

"I don't know if I could do three things at once where you're involved."

"Three?"

"Making love to you while driving a car that's a stick shift? Pretty tricky."

We finally arrived at the Long Warf Marriott in Boston at around nine. I had told her we would stay in on Friday night but Saturday night was a fancy night out. I grabbed her garment bag with mine and checked into the hotel. Sitting on the counter was a dozen red roses in a vase. The card said Chelsea Michaels on the outside. I was a little puzzled because I hadn't ordered them. Saturday was her twenty-eighth birthday so I imagined they were from her parents.

"Those are for you." I said nodding at the flowers.

She opened the envelope and lost some color in her face. She put the card back in the envelope and smiled at me.

"Who are they from?" I asked.

"No one." She said, "Is our room ready?"

"Chelsea," I warned, "who are they from?"

"They're from me," answered a tall blonde from behind her. If possible, her face was even paler. She closed her eyes and shook her head.

"Dr. Steven Edwards." He said putting out his hand for me to shake.

I shook his hand, "Payne Williams." Chelsea finally turned around with a taut smile on her face.

"Hi Steve." She said not moving to shake his hand or embrace him in anyway.

He leaned forward and kissed her cheek. "Happy Birthday Chelsea."

"Thanks. How did you know I was here?"

"I knew you had a signing at the Barnes and Noble. I asked Tommy where you were staying. When the florist said you didn't have a room here I decided to come over and wait."

I made a mental note to kill her brother.

"Well thanks for coming but I'm booked pretty solid this weekend." She said giving him the cold shoulder. "Maybe next time you're in New York you can give us a call."

She turned and walked away with the room key in her hand leaving me alone with Steve. The flowers lay unclaimed on the counter. I picked up my garment bag and overnight case in preparation to follow her.

"Well then. It was nice to meet you." I said to him. "I really think it would be best if you left her alone. She's moved on and if you really cared about her you'd let her go."

I walked after her leaving Steve behind with his unclaimed roses. I finally caught up to her in the elevator bank. She was sitting down in a wingback chair waiting for me. Her bags were at her feet and her head was in her hands. I stopped in front of her. She looked up at me.

"I am so embarrassed." She said. "I'm sorry. The only way to deal with Steve is to walk away." She finally got up from her chair.

"I really hope he doesn't give us a call next time he's in New York. Because it took all I had to not deck him in the middle of the lobby. I wanted nothing better than to beat the snot out of him but finding you was more important. I told him that if he really cared about you that he should leave you alone."

"Thanks." She said picking up her bag. That's when I noticed her hands were trembling. "Can we please just get upstairs and call it a night?"

"We can do anything you want to do." I said with a smile.

She stood up and kissed me. I pressed the up button for the elevator. We rode the elevator to the sixth floor. I had asked for a room with a view of Boston Harbor. I wasn't disappointed. She walked in and immediately chastised me.

"You paid way too much for this room." She said. "It's beautiful." She went right to the window and looked out at the harbor. I went up behind her and put my arms around her. She leaned back into me happy to look out at the water. Across the bay was Logan Airport. An occasional plane took off from a runway.

"Happy Birthday Chelsea." I said kissing the top of her head. She turned in my arms.

"Thank you." She said kissing me. "Whatever else you have planned for the weekend doesn't really matter. What you did in the lobby was the best present ever."

"Oh no I have more tricks up my sleeve." I said with a smile.

"So do I." She laughed and pulled me over to the bed.

"Promise?" I asked. She pulled me down on the bed and began pulling at my clothes. Before I knew it she had my shirt off and pants off. I was lying on my back in my boxers. She got up from the bed and went over to her overnight bag. She came over with her hands behind her back.

"Roll over on your stomach." She said. "Please."

I rolled over. I heard the rustle of her clothes coming off and she crawled up the king size bed. She ran her hands up the inside of my legs. I jumped.

"Relax." She said next to my ear. I could feel the tips of her breasts brush against my back. She had removed her clothes.

"Easier said than done." I said as she squeezed lotion onto my back. It was cold and I jumped again.

"Sorry. It's been in the car all day. It will warm up soon." She bent down next to my ear. "I promise."

She began to work the lotion into my back muscles. In college she had worked in the athletic training room. She had learned to massage sore muscles. I had benefited briefly in the second year we were dating from her training room work. It had been a long time since I had a decent massage. She was right about the lotion, it began to heat up as she worked it into my skin. She eased down my boxers and even found knots in my butt. I was completely relaxed. She stretched out on top of me and whispered in my ear, "Do you want a happy ending?"

I rolled over pulling her with me. I was now on top of her and pushed inside her. "Do you want a happy ending?" I asked her.

"Don't all women want a happy ending?" She laughed as I moved inside her. Pretty soon she couldn't concentrate on anything else but our movements. I rolled over again and she was on top of me. She had once told me she felt really uncomfortable on top. With such large breasts, the movements would always make them bounce too much. She was moving slowly and my hands moved up to cup her breasts. I brought my thumbs across her nipples and pulled her down to kiss her.

"Do you want to go for a ride?" I asked her against her lips.

She smiled and leaned back. She was moving up and down at different speeds. She would speed up and then lean forward and slow down. I lay there and watched the emotions across her face. She was unsure of herself at times and looked down at my face for some kind of guidance. I would reach up and pull her down for a kiss. I would thrust up inside her as she moved down and she would groan. When she was in fevered pitch moving fast, I couldn't take anymore. I rolled her over onto her back. I hooked my right arm under her left leg and pushed into her the last few times. She screamed with the release.

I collapsed on top of her. I rose up on my elbows and looked at her. She looked completely exhausted. Her eyes would close for a few moments and then open to find me smiling at her. She would smile back.

"Happy Birthday." I said stroking her cheek. "I love you."

I waited for her to respond in kind. Her eyes were closed and she was clearly asleep. I had taken the time the last few weeks to buy her multiple birthday presents. There were eight different presents; one for each year I had missed. The first one was a Fairfield University T-Shirt. I knew she would get up in the morning to get a workout in. I got out of bed and pulled the first wrapped present out of my bag. I left the wrapped t-Shirt on the counter in the bathroom. The card read simply "Happy Twentieth Birthday."

I lay down on the bed and pulled Chelsea into my arms. She was sleeping soundly which was odd for her. I turned on the TV. I immediately found ESPN and watched the recap at eleven. I fell asleep sometime after that.

CHAPTER 22

❀

Payne was sleeping on his stomach with one hand still clutching the remote. The clock said seven. I eased out of bed and turned off the TV. I walked in the bathroom to find a simple white shirt box with a red bow. The card very simply said, "Happy Twentieth Birthday, Love Payne." I looked at the card several times. I opened the box to find a Fairfield University Soccer T-Shirt. I laughed and changed into my workout clothes. I went over to the bed and bent to kiss Payne.

"Thanks sweetie." I said.

"Your welcome." He said, "Going for a workout downstairs?"

"Yeah. I should be back in about an hour." I told him, "Signing is at eleven on Washington Street."

"OK. I'm going to catch some more sleep." He closed his eyes and was asleep before I left the room.

I found the workout room easily and ran for forty-five minutes on the treadmill. It was a nice release from stress. I hadn't expected Steve to show up. It really shook me. If I had been in Boston alone it would not have been an issue. That Payne was there to witness my first run-in with Steve was what made me nervous. I was afraid of what Steve would do. I was hoping that Payne wasn't planning to be at the signing today. I didn't want a scene at the Barnes and Noble.

I arrived upstairs to find Payne in shower and the breakfast table set. On the small table in the room was breakfast and on my chair was another white box with a red ribbon. The card said, "Happy Twenty-frist Birthday. Love Payne." It was a bottle shaped box. In it was a bottle of Jose Cuervo Gold. I laughed and headed to the bathroom. The shower was still on. I stepped into the shower with Payne. He was shaving.

"Thanks for the Cuervo." I kissed his back. "Do I have to drink it later?"

"Why? You don't drink it anymore?"

"Not since October of junior year. I drank half a bottle and a six pack of beer in two hours." I was washing his back. "I probably should have been in the hospital THAT night. But I just puked my brains out and went to bed. It was the following weekend that I ended up in the emergency room."

He turned around and hugged me to him. "Did you have a good work out?"

"I had a nice run." I answered, "They didn't have a rower." I reached up on tiptoe and kissed him.

"Breakfast is getting cold." He said kissing me as he moved around me to get out.

"Do you really care?" I asked as I kissed his neck.

"No." He said as I began to move further down his body. I pushed him up against the tile. I was kneeling in front of him with the water beating down on me.

His hands were in my hair as I took his penis in my mouth. It was always a challenge to keep him completely in my mouth. The water streaming down my back added a challenge to breathing. I looked up at one point to see Payne's head back against the tiled wall and his eyes closed in ecstasy. I moved my hands up his inner thighs and it was too much for him. He pulsed into my mouth with a groan.

I stood up kissing his stomach as I made my way up to his mouth. I kissed him quickly on the mouth. I turned my face into the water and began to shampoo my hair. I turned to rinse it and he was gone. I finished up in the shower quickly and got out to join him. He was seated on the bed with his boxers on. He had a pair of jeans around his ankles and pulled them up as I walked in. He turned to me and smiled.

"What time is the signing?" he asked pulling on his shirt.

"Eleven. What's wrong?" I asked. Something was definitely wrong.

"Jim called. He has orders for deployment in four weeks. He'll leave right before Christmas. I'm a little off." He said as he sat down to eat breakfast.

"Wow." I said sitting down across from him. "That's scary. I don't know what I would do if you.…"

"If I what?" he interrupted.

"If you were going off to war. I worry about you now. I can't imagine how much I would worry with you in a war zone." I was looking at my plate. I had eaten most of the food on it.

"Please don't worry about me. It's a job and I'm good at what I do." He reached out to cover my hand.

I nodded my head. It was the closest I had come to telling him how much he meant to me. I finished eating and put on my clothes. I turned around to find him lying on the bed watching me get ready. I smiled and asked, "How do I look?"

"Beautiful as always. Wait you're missing something". He reached in the nightstand and pulled out a thin long box with a red ribbon. "This might fix that"

I sat down on the bed with him. The card on the box said Happy Twenty-second Birthday. Love Payne. I opened the box to find a sterling silver charm bracelet with a heart attached to it. It was engraved with his initials. PFW.

I began to cry. "Thank you so much. Really Payne this is all too much." I unclasped the bracelet and put it on my right hand. "You're setting the bar way too high for me. What am I get you when you turn thirty in March?"

"I don't know. I'll think of something." He said. "Come on we need to get going. I'm going to go with you to the signing, but I may duck out for a few minutes to take care of some things. If Steve shows up, you call me on my cell. That's not open for discussion."

We left the hotel together and headed to the Barnes and Noble on Washington Street. There was a large crowd. Payne deposited me at the table but then disappeared for about half an hour. I was preoccupied with watching the door. I was nervous that Steve would show up and more anxious about Payne returning. I was speaking to an elderly lady about plans for another book when I saw Steve come in. What I hadn't seen was Payne returning just before him. Before I knew it, Payne was leading Steve to the alcove that housed the restrooms. Unfortunately I couldn't leave the table. I had a long line of people waiting to have their books signed. I kept one eye on the alcove. Steve came out first and headed quickly out the front door. Payne soon came out and walked directly toward me. He didn't seem happy at all. He walked behind me, leaned in and whispered, "We need to talk later."

I nodded and signed my name to another book. I was convinced he would leave but he didn't. He settled into a chair and began to read the paper. I continued signing the books through two. At that point, I stood up from the table and headed toward Payne. I sat down on the arm of the chair. He looked up at me and I saw the hurt in his eyes. For the first time since he walked into my classroom six weeks ago, I saw what I had done to him by not telling him the whole story.

"Why didn't you tell me about the baby?" He asked.

CHAPTER 23

After Chelsea left for her workout, my day started off very badly. My cell phone rang. It was Jim. He was calling during a break at drill.

"Hey what's up?" I asked.

"I'm headed out in four weeks." He said simply. "It sucks. I'm not even seeing any real action. It's a bullshit diplomatic mission. Some fucking guard-duty-opening-door bullshit mission."

"Man that sucks." I said. As much as he was upset about not seeing any action, I was relieved. He was an excellent shot; the best in the Philadelphia office but you can't shoot a roadside bomb. "Are you still coming up on Wednesday?"

"Definitely. Let's do the town. I'll have to head down to Atlanta the weekend after to see my family. How's it going with you? Phase two working?"

"So far so good. We arrived here last night to find her ex-boyfriend waiting for her. I have to have a few words with her brother Tommy about that one. Listen I've got to get going. I have to order room service and set up the next gift. I'll call you on Tuesday to get the details for Thanksgiving weekend."

"You got it." Jim said hanging up.

I was more than a little off with the news that Jim would be deployed in four weeks. He seemed really tough on the outside but was very sensitive. I was afraid of what a deployment would do to him. I called in room service and had her present all set up. I jumped in the shower and was pleasantly interrupted by Chelsea.

I had given her the engraved heart but her statements nagged me. The first one was something I didn't understand. The weekend before she overdosed she drank half a bottle of tequila and a six-pack of beer in two hours. She never really drank that much especially during crew season. It made me rethink her nonchalant attitude toward her accidental overdose. Had it really be an accident? I then thought about her concern for me. She worried about me. That was a good sign. She was thinking about buying me something for my thirtieth birthday. That was another good sign. But I kept thinking about the binge on Cuervo right before she overdosed. I needed to piece things together. I needed a timeline.

I needed to run some errands while she was signing books. I had checked the location of the Barnes and Noble and knew that I would be able to get the things that I needed close by. There was one present I had planned that I couldn't sneak into the car for the weekend. I stopped at the Bath and Body Works that was by the Barnes and Noble and had them put together a small basket of goodies for her. I then had the store deliver it to my room at the hotel. I had just walked into the bookstore and had made my way to the newspaper rack when I saw Steve come in.

I approached him, "Could I have a word with you in private?"

"Sure," he said following me into the alcove by the bathrooms.

"I really thought that I had made myself clear last night when I told you to let go." I was less than pleasant in my tone.

"I understand but you have to know what she is like. I'm not about to give up without a fight. Is that what you're spoiling for? A fight?"

"I really don't want to be that juvenile about it." I said. "As for knowing what she is like, I've known Chelsea ten years, and I know more about her than you do."

"Do you?" He said getting angry. "Do you really?"

"Yeah I do." I said getting just as angry. "She loves me."

"Sure she does. She's loved you since she met you, and you left her. You left her alone and pregnant. She was so alone she tried to kill herself not once but twice."

"What! What are you talking about? She wasn't pregnant. She'd been on the pill for almost two years. She accidentally overdosed on sleeping pills one night."

"So you know her do you? Do you know she miscarried the baby the night she overdosed? Do you know what day that was? It was October sixteenth. A year ago, seven years later, that same day, she came home drunk and fell in bed with me. I held her that night while she cried. And where were you the last seven years when she was tortured once a year by her loss?"

I was struck by this information. I was silent while he continued.

"So you listen to me," Steve continued, "Tommy doesn't know about the baby. As much as I'd love to tell him, which would lead to the beating you so deserve, she loves you too much. And I can't understand why. She had driven five hours to talk to you about the baby only to find out you were screwing someone else. She came home and drank herself into oblivion. Then there was the overdose and the miscarriage. So you know her? She never told you. But she told me."

"I'm back to stay Steve. I'm going to make it right. I'm going to marry her. Not because I feel sorry for her, but because I love her. And she loves me."

"Has she told you she loves you?" He asked. From the look on my face he knew the answer. "I didn't think so. She can't say it.

Don't expect her to say it because she told me she wouldn't say it again. Ever. Tommy told me he already threatened your life. Let me make myself really clear. What Tommy will do to you won't come close to what I'll do to you if you break her heart again."

He walked away from me careful not to look at Chelsea. I wasn't so lucky. I couldn't bring myself to stop staring at her.

I walked over to her and leaned down behind her to whisper, "We need to talk later." She nodded. She continued to sign the books, but I could tell she was wondering what we needed to talk about.

I sat down with the newspaper. My mind was spinning so fast I couldn't concentrate on anything. A baby. She had been pregnant and never told me. She needed to tell me. I needed to hear these things from her not her ex-boyfriend. She was finally finished and came over to me. She sat on the arm of my chair. I looked up at her. The betrayal and sadness was in my eyes. I was close to tears.

"Why didn't you tell me about the baby?" I asked.

She let out her breath. "Can we go for a walk to talk about this?"

"Sure." I said. I grabbed my coat. I waited for her to get her coat from the front desk. We walked out the door and began walking back toward the Long Warf. I waited for her to speak. I couldn't speak. There was a lump in my throat.

"At the end of September our junior year, I found out I was six weeks pregnant. I had been taking antibiotics in August and didn't know that they would make the pill ineffective. I knew we were having problems. I didn't want to tell you over the phone. I drove down to see you and found out about Tracey."

We had reached the Long Warf. She sat down on a bench. "I couldn't bring myself to tell you about the baby. I knew you would want to get married. I didn't want you to be stuck with me and resent me. I had decided to have the baby and figure things out. I drove back to school that weekend and was talked into going out to a party. I was so depressed and I started drinking and I couldn't stop. I threw up and passed out. The following week I bought some sleeping pills." She had begun to cry. I was standing in front of her but I couldn't look her in the face. Instead, I was staring at a boat in the water behind her.

"I had no one to talk to. You had your new life. I had a few friends but no one I could really talk to about this desire I had to kill myself. I started taking sleeping pills. I overdosed and went into labor. When I said I didn't wake up for the second fire alarm it was due to two things. I had too much alcohol and pills in me and I had begun to bleed. I hadn't told anyone I was pregnant. I still haven't told anyone about the baby. I told my therapist but not another soul until last year. I told Steve."

"Why Steve?" I asked.

"I don't know. I came home drunk and I fell in bed with him. October sixteenth is always a difficult day. I try to stay as busy as possible so I don't think about it. I had a difficult day at school that day. They were planning the Right to Life march for January. It made me think of that little baby I didn't have. I felt so selfish for trying to kill myself. It brought it all back. I started drinking on the subway and didn't stop until I was home. Steve was home and heard me crying. He came up to my room and it just happened."

"Why didn't you tell me?" I asked. "There have been so many times you could have told me. So many times."

"I didn't want to hurt you." She said softly

"That didn't quite work they way you planned it did it?"

"No." She said even softer. "I'm sorry."

"So am I." I said. "So am I." I began to walk away. I walked further down the wharf. There was nowhere to go. I was almost at the end when I heard her call out to me.

"Payne." She called. "Please don't leave. I …"

I turned to her angry and saddened. I wasn't going to leave. I just needed some time to digest it all. "He was right. You can't say it. You can't say you love me. Even when you think it would make me stay, you can't say it. I'll say it for you. I love you. Even after you hurt me, I still love you."

She had her face buried in her hands. She was sobbing. I pulled her into my arms and then sat down on a bench pulling her with me. "Shh." I said. "I'm not going to stop loving you Chelsea. You need to trust me. I'm not walking away. Not now. Not ever."

She had stopped crying and was shuddering. "I have a few more gifts to give you before the night is over. You can relax. One of them is not an engagement ring. I don't want to rush you. You take your time, but I need to get you off my lap pretty soon or I won't be able to walk. Or I'll be frozen to this bench."

She slid off my lap and I stood. I pulled her up to stand in front of me. She still wouldn't look at me. I tipped her chin up and waited for her to look me in the eyes. "Are we starting over?"

She nodded. "So let's get ready for a new start tonight." I said.

We walked up to the room. On the bed was the basket of bath goods. She opened the card and smiled. I had walked into the bathroom and turned on the bathwater for her. She brought the basket in.

"Thank you."

"You need to relax. Take a really a long bath. I'll check on you in about half an hour. OK?"

She nodded and began to get undressed for her bath. After about half an hour, I walked into the bathroom to check on her. She was asleep with her head on a bath pillow. I leaned down and kisser her. "Wake up sleeping beauty. We need to get moving."

She stretched and I handed her a towel. She stepped out of the tub and I grabbed her to me. She put her head on my shoulder and I held her for a few moments. I dragged her out into the hotel room to reveal her next few presents. Laid out on the bed were a series of boxes. She opened them in order. The first was a set of black lace underwear complete with a garter belt and stockings. The box next to it was small. I saw her pause. It was close to the same size as a ring box.

"It's close but not what you think." She opened the diamond earrings. "Twenty-five is a grown up birthday. So I got grown up earrings for you."

The next box was a high-necked black dress that went to the floor, but had a slit up to the knee. The last box was a hand knit Irish stole.

"Are we going out tonight?" She asked.

"Yes and I'm not telling you where."

I quickly put on my suit and sat at the table and chairs to watch her get dressed. It was something I could do for hours. She finished her underwear and was moving onto the dress. Finally she was dressed and her hair and make up done. I checked my watch. It was a quarter to five. We had fifteen minutes before our reservation for dinner.

"Are you ready?" I asked.

She nodded. I could tell she was still apprehensive about the afternoon's events. I reminded her of our agreement. "Fresh start. Right?"

She smiled, "Fresh start. Does that mean I don't have to put out tonight?"

"You forget. You put out on our first date."

"I know. You just do something to me that I can't explain."

"Good to know." I said as I pulled the door open. We made our way down to the lobby.

"We don't need the car do we?"

"No we're walking."

CHAPTER 24

✣

We walked out the hotel lobby onto the wharf. Payne steered me out toward the water. There was only one restaurant out this far. It was the Chart House. I stopped.

"Don't tell me you made reservations at the Chart House." He had continued to walk but turned back to me and smiled.

"OK. I didn't make reservations at he Chart House, but its too cold out here to have this conversation. Let's go to the Chart House and discuss how I didn't make reservations there."

"Payne. You have spent entirely too much money as it is. You're crazy."

"There's that fine line in law enforcement isn't there. Maybe I've stepped over the line." We were at the Chart House doors. He opened them for me. He did in fact have a reservation.

We sat at our table. I was reluctant to order things because the prices were so high. I think he knew what was going on in my mind. "Stop worrying." He said. "Can I guess what you like?"

"Give it a try." I laughed.

"Coconut shrimp to start, a salad and sea scallops and definitely the hot chocolate lava cake. White wine definitely. You're so much more fun when you have a nice buzz going."

I laughed. He had picked exactly what I wanted. I was thinking twice about some of the order due to the prices on the menu. He took the option away and ordered for me when the waiter arrived.

Payne wasn't as big a fish eater as I was. He chose the lobster rolls with a filet and shrimp combination. He didn't order a desert and had red wine with dinner.

"What did Jim have to say?" I asked.

"He's mad as hell. He wants to go overseas and knock some heads together. Unfortunately, he has a degree in international relations and surprisingly hasn't been tapped before this. It's what did he call it a 'fucking guard-duty-opening-door bullshit mission.' All the same I'd rather see him on that than with daily combat."

"How long has he been in the guard?" I asked.

"Forever. He joined in high school and stayed in through college and even now. I think he's a captain now. After this deployment he'll probably be a major."

"Are you worried about him?"

"Yes and no. He's an excellent shot. Best in the Philly department, but you can't shoot a roadside bomb. I worry about the little stuff that can go wrong. He didn't tell me much about the mission but even diplomatic missions aren't safe."

"Is he still coming up for Thanksgiving?" I asked

"He wouldn't miss it for the world. He's driving my car up on Wednesday after work."

"I'm not working that day. We're closed. Have him come to my house. You can meet me there and I'll drive my car back to my parents' house. There's a great bar in Hicksville that I want to take you both to. Especially Jim. Thanksgiving is an all day thing at my parents' house. We can take the train back to your place to go out on Friday night. You do have off on Friday?"

"I'm on call Friday and Saturday during the day for anything that may come up but I'll be good to go on Friday night."

"Where do you think Jim will want to go?"

"What's that bar that didn't let women in for a while? The Irish place that throws you out for not drinking fast enough?"

I laughed. "McSorley's. It's a huge tourist attraction but a lot of fun. Any place else."

"This is going to sound really scary but a club of some kind. Once Jim is tanked he loves to dance."

"Is he any good?" I asked trying to get a visual.

"As good as anyone his size can be." He laughed. "He has perfected the butt smacking move. It's pretty funny to watch."

I was laughing so hard I was crying. "Stop!" I said between fits of laughter.

He was sitting back in his chair watching me laugh. He had a warm smile across his face. I calmed myself down and went back to eating.

"I love to watch you laugh." He said. "It makes me happy to see you laugh. I especially love it when I am the one who makes you laugh."

I smiled at him, "You've always made me happy. I hope that you can say the same."

"Chelsea. You undoubtedly have made me a happy man. Multiple times. Sometimes in one night."

I kicked him under the table. "I'm serious. Do I make you happy?"

He looked at me seriously. "Yes. There's only one way to make me even happier. Tell me you love me."

I looked down at my plate. The hot chocolate lava cake was sitting there. I suddenly couldn't eat it. I put my fork down.

He reached across and squeezed my hand. "I'm also a patient man. I know that when you tell me you love me, you'll mean it."

I looked up at him and smiled weakly. "Why do you put up with me?"

"Because I love you." He said simply, "Are you finished?"

"Yes." I said, "What's next?"

"You'll see."

We walked out of the Chart House and crossed the streets to the Quincy Market area. In front of the Black Rose Irish Pub there were carriage rides. Payne paid for a ride and we got in. The ride takes you around the Quincy Market area. The carriage driver gave facts about certain buildings. We were snuggled under a heavy blanket. Payne's hand began to slide up my leg. He leaned closer to me. "I'm sorry I was looking for something else."

"What exactly were you looking for?" I asked moving my leg closer to him.

He reached into his suit pocket and pulled out a small flat jewelry case. "I was looking for this but I'll certainly take what I found by accident."

"Happy Birthday." He said as he handed me the signature blue Tiffany box. I opened the white ribbon. Inside was a diamond circle pendant.

I was surprised and at the same time thrilled. I leaned into him and kissed him. "Thank you."

He had already moved his hand up my skirt and was stroking the skin above my stocking. "You're welcome." He said watching me as I closed my eyes in pleasure. Before I knew it we were back at the start of the ride. When we stepped out of the carriage, I was immediately chilled.

"Do you want a drink?" He asked. I nodded.

We walked into the Black Rose. It was perhaps the best-known Irish bar in Boston. They almost always had live music. We walked in and were lucky to get a table down front. There was an Irish singer performing that night. She was singing an acoustic set when we came in. After we had taken our seats, she began a song called "Beside Me."

I've got my baby beside me
I've got his strong arms to hide me
Confusion cannot deny me
This love I have inside me

I love you with wild abandon
I need you more than I ever show
You've touched somewhere deep inside me
I love you that's all I know

I love the way you love watching me loving you
You never take your eyes off me
I'm happy to fall asleep in your arms
Happy with my love beside me

I've got my baby beside me

The words called out to me. They echoed the last six weeks with Payne. It seemed I could do anything if he was beside me. We stayed for a few drinks and we walked back to Marriott Long Wharf. When we walked into the room, the light on the phone was flashing that there were messages. Payne knew most of them were for me. They were any number of messages from my family wishing me happy birthday. Tommy, my parents, and Susan all called to wish me a happy birthday. Payne waited patiently for me to go through the messages.

"Anyone good?" He asked when I was finished. I joined him on the bed. He was sitting with his back against the headboard and I climbed between his legs sitting with my back to his front.

"Mom and Dad, Susan, and Tommy." I said.

"I need to have a talk with Tommy at Thanksgiving." Payne said. "You should too. Steve told me that Tommy doesn't know about the baby. You need to tell him. I don't want Steve holding that over our heads."

"I'll talk to Tommy. What did Steve say to you?" I asked.

"He told me you lost the baby on October sixteenth. That's the day I found you in your classroom working late. It took me most of the day to put that together."

I nodded. "I try to keep myself busy that day. It's a very difficult day for me. I was working late trying to avoid being home alone and thinking about it when you walked into my room."

"You'll never be alone that day again. I swear. Steve pretty much ripped me a new asshole. He's a huge fan yours; not such a fan of me. What did you tell him about me?"

"I was so drunk I don't even remember. I know I told him I caught you cheating and that I had been pregnant. I told him about the two suicide attempts. Apparently that's enough."

"He told me you loved me. He told me you still love me but you'll never say it again. He also told me if I broke your heart again, what Tommy did to me would be considered a vacation in comparison to what he would do to me."

I flinched. "Sorry. I don't know why they feel the need to be that way."

"Because you have a soft heart. Any other woman would have slapped me across the face when I appeared at her door eight years after I had gotten her pregnant, cheated on her, and broke up with her. You. You gave me a hug, went out to dinner with me, took me home, and fucked me."

I smacked his arm. "You gave me your business card and set up a possible second date. If you could call our night at the Gingerman and your house a date. You are definitely one in a million and I can't blame Steve for the one last ditch effort to get you back."

"I really made it clear to him in June that I only wanted to be friends." I was frowning.

"So tell me." He said turning my head to look at him. "What's he like in bed?"

"Payne, I'm not answering that!" I said. I blushed. "What's Gina like in bed?"

"Terrible. Boring. She sure wouldn't let me cover her with otter pops and strawberries."

I was silent.

"I'm waiting." He said. When I still didn't answer, he prodded even more. "That good."

"That bad. He was always too tired to have sex. Even when we had sex, it was less than wonderful. My heart wasn't in it."

"I guess I am as Jim says, 'one lucky bastard.'" He said gloating.

"And?" I asked. I was curious.

"And what?" He asked."

"Payne really how can you be so dense?" I began. I couldn't look at him. Then I noticed he was shaking with laughter. I tried to get up and he rolled me over and pinned me to the bed.

"Chelsea," He said, "of all the women I've been with.…"

"How many?"

"Ten."

"Really only ten?" I was quickly adding in my mind. That meant that between our separations he hadn't been as busy as I would have thought. I was number four. I knew about the three before me. I knew about two of the six after me.

"Of all the women I've been with, I've never wanted to go back for seconds once we ended. You are the only one I've come back to. You're the only one for me. I don't know how I can convince you of that."

"I've never really been good with math. I was four. Tracey was five. Can you fill in the other five? Gina's in there somewhere?"

"I'm not really proud of this but six, seven, and eight were all one night stands. Gina was number nine."

"Who was number ten?" I asked. I was trying to figure it out in my mind. He must have cheated on Gina. It made me a little nervous.

"Some girl I met in New York city."

I stiffened. He laughed and rolled me onto my back. Stretched out on top of me, he explained. "You are number ten. I thought you said we were starting over tonight. You are a different person than you were eight years ago and I love you even more."

He lay on top of me waiting. "And? Is there anyone else I should worry about in New York that wants to kick my ass to get you back into his bed?"

"No. There's only one other guy and he's married now with three kids. I was his last fling so to speak. He was my first test in bed after you. I wanted to see if it was as good with someone else."

"Did you get your answer?" He seemed nervous.

"No."

"No you didn't get your answer or the answer was no?

"No, it was never as good as it is with you." He looked relieved and proud at the same time. What a male ego.

"Do you know how lucky we are? What are the odds that we would find each other? What are the odds that we would come back to each other?"

"I don't know. What are the odds we'll stay together?" I was still worried about the future.

"Pretty good if you ask me. I always bet on the odds. Speaking of odds. Are you sure you're not going to get pregnant again while on the pill?"

"Odds are against it. Would it be such a bad thing? Unlike before, I would love to have your baby."

"Not in my eyes. I'd love for you to have my baby too, but you might have some explaining to do at work."

I pressed my hips up against him. "Want to beat the odds?"

"I've always been one to gamble; especially when I have an ace up my sleeve."

"I don't know about your sleeve, but I think there's definitely an ace in your pants." I said with a laugh.

"Really bad." He said grinding his hips into me. "But very true."

CHAPTER 25

Wednesday evening, Jim arrived at Chelsea's house around six. He was overly affectionate toward Chelsea. He got out of the car and immediately hugged her to his very large body.

"Jim." I warned him. "You need to put her down before you won't be able to go to Iraq."

"Dude. You've got to cut me some slack. I'm headed to the sandbox where all the girls are either all covered up or nasty looking. Your girl is the best thing this side of heaven."

He finally put her down. Chelsea took his bag out of the back of the civic and put it in the Jeep.

"She drives a Jeep?" Jim asked. "I'm so in love with her."

"She has that effect on men. I know it sucks, but we've got to hit the road to her parents' house."

"Let me take a leak first." Jim followed Chelsea in the back door to the bathroom. When he returned we climbed into the Jeep. I elected to drive. Chelsea hopped in the back out of respect for our height.

"How was Boston?" Jim asked.

"Great!" Chelsea said. "It was like Christmas. Payne's setting me up for a difficult time when he turns thirty in March."

"Tell me about your family." Jim said.

"My dad's finally retired. He was head of security at Molloy College until about three years ago. He was a Navy man. He served in the Reserves until about five years ago. He's big like you but less muscle than you and more fat. My mom's a saint. She puts up with his crap as well as my brother Tommy."

"Is Tommy going to be there tonight?" I asked looking at her in the rear view mirror.

"No. We'll be saved his presence until Thanksgiving Day. Listen to me Payne. I get to talk to him first."

"Fine." I said.

"This should be fun. I haven't had a good dysfunctional holiday in a few years." Jim commented with a laugh.

Chelsea laughed. "There's definitely going to be some tension this weekend. But none of it is your fault. Most of it is my fault. You, in fact, are our huge distraction. So thanks in advance."

"What's the plan for tonight?" Jim asked.

"We'll grab a late dinner at my parents. We should be there around eight. My mom is sure to have lasagna made for us. At around nine or ten we could head out to Jackie Reilly's."

"I love a good Irish bar." Jim said.

"This place is the best. Sean, the owner used to tend bar at the Wantagh Inn not that far from the beach. He was the best bar tender in the world. You will witness a master in action tonight."

"I'm up for anything. I'm headed to places without alcohol. I need to stock up on the memories to get me through the dry spell."

I laughed. "They won't give you leave in … what's that country called?"

"Qatar. No it's too short of a deployment. Anyway, they ration the beers so it pretty much sucks. I'll be a two beer sally when I get back from active duty."

"Friday night we're heading out in Manhattan. We'll start at McSorley's. You'll love that place. They throw you out if you don't drink fast enough."

"Can I tell you again how priceless she is?" He said to Payne.

"Feel free to tell me in front of her every chance you get. Maybe it will remind her that I'm not letting her go this time."

"Jim," Chelsea asked, "Are you headed down to Atlanta to see your family?"

"Next weekend when the crowds in the airport calm down."

"Who's at home?" Chelsea asked Jim

"My mom. My dad died about ten years ago and two of my five brothers still live in the Atlanta area. I'll see my mom at least."

"Leaving anyone special behind?" Chelsea prodded.

"No. That's what will make this weekend so much fun." Jim said laughing. We touched fisted knuckles over that prospect.

We made good time out to Hicksville. I could tell Chelsea was nervous about brining me home again. I was nervous about not proving myself worthy to her family. We all grabbed our bags and Chelsea led the way to the front door. Most of the houses in Hicksville were small capes. Her parents' house was an exception. While their house was a cape, they had made extensive renovations on the house to make it larger than the average house. I had been there before the renovations and I couldn't believe it was the same house. What had once been a small living room and dining room was now one big open family room. They had expanded the kitchen into the backyard creating a new dining room. Her father was sitting in his favorite chair watching TV when we walked in. He stood. Chelsea went over to him and gave him a big hug and kiss. He was still the bear of a man I remembered just older.

"Hi Daddy." She said, "You remember Payne and this is his friend Jim Collins." We moved forward to shake his hand. He took my offered hand which I looked at as hopeful. Before the end of the day tomorrow I would definitely know where I stood with him.

"Payne." He said as he shook my hand. "Pleasure to meet you Jim. Chelsea tells me you're an army man."

"Yes sir. Fifteen years in the National Guard."

"It's a pleasure. She says you're headed overseas in a few weeks."

"Yes sir. I'd be looking forward to it more if it wasn't such sissy assignment."

"Young man. I don't think any deployment is a sissy assignment. Why don't you guys head into the kitchen and get some dinner before Chelsea takes you out to Jackie Reilly's."

The three of us started moving into the kitchen. Chelsea's father called her to stay behind. I could overhear him say to her. "No funny business in my house. You stay in your room and the boys sleep in the basement." I chuckled. If he only knew the funny business that went on his basement almost ten years ago he wouldn't let me in his home.

Chelsea was a carbon copy of her mother. Her mother in her parents' wedding picture was almost identical to Chelsea. Walking into the kitchen, I smiled because if Chelsea looked this good thirty years from now, I would continue to be a happy man.

"Hello Mrs. Michaels." I said in greeting.

She paused in stirring the pot on the stove. The kitchen smelled of garlic and tomato sauce. "Hello Payne." She stepped away from the stove to hug me. "It's good to see you again. You brought a friend with you. I'm Colleen Michaels."

"It's a pleasure to meet you ma'am. I'm Jim Collins. Thank you very much for having us for Thanksgiving."

"The centerpiece arrived earlier today Payne. It's beautiful and unnecessary."

"No it was very necessary. Thanks for having us."

"Sit down and have something to eat." She went over to the stove as Chelsea walked in.

"Hi mom." Chelsea said to her mom. She gave her a big hug and kiss. "Did you meet Jim?"

"Yes dear. Can you grab the boys plates while I get the lasagna out of the oven?"

Chelsea grabbed our plates off the table and brought them over to her mom at the stove. She put a healthy piece of lasagna and meatballs. Chelsea grabbed three cans of Pepsi out of the refrigerator and brought them over to the table.

"Nice necklace Chelsea. Where did you get that?" her mother asked.

"Payne bought it for my for my birthday." She said beaming.

"We'll I must say Payne, you have excellent taste in jewelry." Mrs. Michaels said.

After eating, Chelsea led us to the basement. Jim and I had been assigned the queen-sized sofa couch.

"My mom put fresh sheets on it today." Chelsea said.

"May I remind you how much I love your parents' couch bed?" I said grabbing Chelsea and kissing her.

"Stop it." She said looking up at the stairs. She whispered, "My father already gave me a stern warning. You and Jim are to stay in the basement and I'm in my bedroom upstairs. The 'There's no funny business in my house' speech."

I laughed. "If he only knew."

"Don't you dare! Might I remind you of the VERY large hole you need to dig yourself out of with my father."

That sobered me. "I know what I'm up against. I won't mess up."

"Who's driving?" Jim asked.

"I'll drive." Chelsea said. "You guys need to blow off some steam."

Chelsea went up to her room to change her clothes while we changed shirts. Jim took the opportunity to ask me about the progress I had been making.

"How do you think things are going?" he asked me.

"It's so funny to hear her say Boston was great. Her ex-boyfriend is such an ass. He shows up Friday night with roses and then after I tell him to leave her alone, he shows up again on Saturday. This time he drops a huge bomb. Basically when Chelsea and I broke up last time, she was six weeks pregnant."

"Did you know?" Jim asked pausing to stare at me.

"Hell no! No one knew. The only reason Steve knew was because she got drunk one night and told him."

"What happened to the baby?" Jim asked.

"She miscarried when she overdosed on sleeping pills."

"Oh man. I'm so sorry."

"Thanks." I said, "It was a shock. We agreed to start over that night. So far so good. I just need to work on her dad and brother."

"That's a tall order. Her father seemed a little cool when we came in."

"Yeah, well he's nothing compared what's going to go down with Tommy. Chelsea's ex-boyfriend is Tommy's best friend and I guess Tommy's the one who told him where we were in Boston. And apparently, Tommy doesn't know about the baby."

Jim whistled. "For the first time since I met Chelsea, I can finally say this. I am SO glad I am not you."

I laughed. "That's what Chelsea meant by getting to talk to him first. She'll put him in his place. You ready?"

Jim nodded and we went up to the living room. Chelsea's dad was watching TV smoking a pipe. We sat on the couch and waited for Chelsea to come downstairs. She came down dressed in knee length jean skirt, a low cut white sweater, and knee-high black boots . Under the sweater was a tank top that revealed a little too much cleavage for my taste. Her hair was up in a simple ponytail.

"Don't wait up for us Dad. Jim's off to the land on no alcohol and no women so you know it will be a late night."

"Tell Sean I said hello." Her father said.

"Good night sir." I said to her father. He nodded his head at us.

We piled into the Jeep and Chelsea drove us to Jackie Reilly's. There was already a good size crowd at the bar. We walked in and Chelsea immediately went up to the bar. A tall gray haired Irishman leaned over and kissed her cheek. I felt a surge of jealousy.

"Ah darlin' you've been away too long. Tommy and your da coming tonight" He said to her.

"No just me. Sorry I've been away. Book stuff." She said.

"Pint of Carlsberg?"

"Can you make it three? I brought some friends tonight." She motioned toward us. We stepped up to the bar.

"This is Payne and Jim. This is the world's best bartender in the world Sean."

"It's a pleasure. Any friend of Chelsea's is welcome here." He extended his hand to us. We shook his hand and sat down at the bar. Chelsea had her one beer and switched to soda. She went to the Jukebox and began to select songs. As we were sitting at the bar, surveying the crowd, our beers were replaced regularly and for every two beers we bought Sean bought us another. Chelsea came back and sat down with a smile.

"You're gonna love the music I picked out." She said with a chuckle. Sean came over to us when she returned to the bar. The crowd had grown considerably and Sean had been busy most of the night.

"So where are you gentlemen from?" Sean asked.

"I'm from Pennsylvania." I volunteered. "Jim here's from Atlanta but lives in Philly."

"Are you visiting?"

"Jim is but I live in Brooklyn."

Chelsea joined the conversation. "They're ATF Seanie. Jim here is headed out to Iraq in four weeks. He's also Army."

"Hooah." Sean said to Jim. Jim smiled. "Might I do something right now."

Sean stepped up onto the bar. He called out to the bar. "Ladies and Gentlemen. This strapping lad is headed overseas shortly to fight for our country. Might you take a moment to raise your glass to him and his fine service to our country? On the count of three raise your glass to and yell Hooah Jim. One. Two. Three."

The entire crowd raised their glasses toward Jim and yelled, "Hooah, Jim."

Jim raised his glass back. Sean was still up on the bar when he added. "Don't bother to buy him his drinks, they're on the house. Go over there and kick some ass."

Sean jumped down on the other side of the bar and clasped Jim in a hug. They were close in size.

"Now that's the way a send off should be done. You keep yourself safe." Sean said. "It's time for me to work the crowd. I promised meself that I'd do that once I owned my own place. I had to wait tonight until the extra staff arrived. Now I get to walk through the crowd groping all the girlies."

We laughed. Chelsea was his first victim. He embraced her in a hug. "So which one of these boys gets to take you home tonight? Please don't say it's the soldier. Not only would I get my ass kicked but I'd feel guilty that I deprived him of your sweet little self before he went off to war."

"That would be me." I said pulling her down on my lap. I couldn't remember how many drinks I has consumed. Sean had done a great job of keeping my glass full.

"Now you take care of my lass." Sean said as he moved away in the crowd.

After Sean made the announcement, numerous people stopped by to wish Jim luck. It became tiresome for him. Most of the crowd was FDNY or NYPD or had someone in the family. After what seemed like forever, Chelsea's selected songs came on. When the first came song came on, I laughed. She had selected "Feel Like Making Love" by Bad Company. Sophomore year at Fairfield, I made the mistake of singing this song at a karaoke night. I would insert Chelsea's name into the chorus. That she didn't break up with me that night I was amazed. At some point, Chelsea took her sweater off and was wearing only her tank top.

"Jesus Chelsea!" I said, "Are you trying to torture me! I have to climb into bed with Jim tonight with no prospect of getting near you."

She walked up to me and stood on the bottom rung of my barstool. She leaned down and kissed me. "You most definitely need to do some penance and tonight would be your night." She slid down the front of me and pulled me off my barstool as her next song came on. It was "Thank You" by Led Zeppelin. She began to sing it to me.

> If the sun refused to shine
> I would still be loving you.
> When mountains crumble to the sea
> There would still be you and me.

She buried her head in my chest and swayed with me. When the song was over a surprising one came on the jukebox. It was the singer Nichola O'Donnell. The one we had seen in Boston last weekend. It would seem logical that another Irish bar would have her CD in the jukebox.

I looked over at Jim. He had about three beers lined up and was looking like he wouldn't be able to stand much longer. I nudged Chelsea's chin. "Babe. I think Jim is done."

She looked over at him and agreed. She put her sweater back on and found Sean. Much the way you wouldn't leave a party without saying good night to the host, there was the air of Jackie Reilly's that you would not leave without saying good-bye to Sean. Chelsea gave him a hug while I shook Sean's hand. Sean gathered Jim to him in a hug telling him to keep safe.

As we walked to the Jeep, Jim pleaded with Chelsea.

"For the love of God, don't do that to me Friday night. I couldn't keep up with the beers and shots people were sending over to me. You'll kill me."

"Sorry. I knew Seanie would hook you up but I didn't think it would be that crazy. You have to admit that was cool."

"Most definitely." Jim said smiling as a drunk could only smile.

"Are you guys hungry?" Chelsea asked.

"Starved." I answered.

"There's a diner around the corner. Do you want to get something to eat?"

We nodded and we headed to the diner. Jim ordered three eggs scrambled with Tabasco sauce. I ordered a club sandwich and Chelsea ordered cheese fries with gravy.

"Cheese fries with gravy?" Jim asked, "I've never heard of that."

"Its awesome." She told him and I agreed.

"Excuse me guys." Chelsea said as she headed to the restroom.

I turned to Jim, "Are you good to sit here for a while?"

Jim smiled and sipped his water.

I followed Chelsea to the restroom to find myself the luckiest man alive. It was a single restroom. I waited outside the door for her. When she opened the door, I pushed my way inside with her

"Payne." She said. "What are you up to?"

I dropped my pants and showed her I was up for anything.

"Are you crazy?" She asked.

I nodded and began pulling at her skirt. It reached her knees and despite the November weather, she hadn't worn any stockings. It didn't take much convincing to get her going.

I picked her up and leaned her up against the door to the bathroom. She was kissing me and I entered her quickly. I knew I had to make it quick before someone wanted to use the bathroom or Jim passed out at the table.

I whispered next to her lips, "Whatever you do, don't scream here. You'll get the biggest crowd, and I think it might get back to your dad." I kept my mouth on top of hers almost the whole time we were having sex. I was almost at the point of no return when someone knocked on the door. I took my mouth away from hers to let her answer.

"Just a minute." She said shakily. I reached down between us and began stroking her with my hands to bring her to orgasm. She groaned and then bit down hard on my shoulder as she shuddered around me. I gave into an unbelievable orgasm. She slid down the door, pulling her skirt down and tossing her panties in the garbage pail while I refastened my jeans. She flushed the toilet and ran the water in the sink as we headed out the door. We were met with a surprised look from a little old lady.

Jim had eaten all of his eggs and was working on my club sandwich and Chelsea's cheese fries.

"Hey guys. Long line at the bathroom?" Jim said with a smile on his face.

Chelsea's face turned bright red. She began eating what was left of her cheese fries.

"Work up an appetite?" He teased Chelsea.

"Jim," I warned, "I wouldn't start with her. She'll finish you."

"Yeah right."

Chelsea picked up a French fry covered with mozzarella cheese dipped it in the gravy and sucked it into her mouth. She began licking her fingers staring right at Jim. Jim didn't know what to do.

"If you must know, Jim, Payne and I were waiting for you to join us. I guess I'll have to sneak into the basement after all." She picked up the pickle from my plate and slid it provocatively into her mouth. "You want some? I won't ask or tell." She bit into the pickle.

Jim was astounded. I put my head back and laughed. Chelsea then burst out in laughter. Jim finally got the joke and laughed.

"Very funny. I don't have anyone to go into the bathroom with me to put me out of my misery."

"Cheer up Jim. I'll find you someone Friday night." Chelsea said. "Wow that sounded a little too much like a pimp."

We all laughed. Chelsea paid the bill and we headed home to her parent's house. It was close to two in the morning. Chelsea kissed me good night in her parents' living room. I went downstairs to the lumpy couch bed and a less than attractive sleeping partner.

Jim took the opportunity to comment one more time on Chelsea. "You fucking lucky bastard. Did you really screw her in the bathroom at the diner?"

"What do you think?" I said laughing.

"She really doesn't have any sisters? Friends?"

I laughed again. "Goodnight Jim." I said and rolled over falling asleep.

CHAPTER 26

I woke up the next morning at eight. I had registered to run a Thanksgiving Day road race at Hicksville High School. I rolled out of bed and threw on my running clothes. I made my way down to the kitchen. My mom was already up and working on Thanksgiving dinner.

"Hey mom." I said.

"Hi sweetie." She said, "What time did you and the boys get in last night?"

"Around two. I'm running the turkey trot race this morning. Only the two-mile race. Do you need anything from the store while I'm out?"

"Why don't you pick up bagels for breakfast? What do you think the boys will want?"

"Aspirin and a lot of water." I laughed.

I ran the two-mile fun run that morning and picked up bagels on the way home from the high school. I made sure to grab two bottles of Pedalyte on the way home. Tommy swore that it was the best thing for a hangover.

I walked in the door to find my dad reading the morning paper. "Hey dad."

"How was the run?" He asked.

"Good. Two more years I get a new age group." I laughed. "The boys up?"

"Not that I heard. What time did you get in?"

"Around two. We went to the diner. Sean says hello. He bought all of Jim's drinks."

My dad laughed. I went down to the basement and found the two of them asleep on opposite edges of the queen-sized sofa bed. I sat down next to Payne and nudged him awake. I put my finger to his lips. He kissed my fingers.

I was in my sports bra and shorts. I hopped in bed between the two of them. Jim was in his t-shirt and the jeans he wore last night. I grabbed his ass. He instantly woke up.

"Hey Jim." I said wiggling my eyebrows at him. "Thanks for a great night." Payne rolled over behind me and pulled me up against him. His early morning erection was pressed against my rear-end.

Jim looked puzzled. "Don't tell me you don't remember." I said. It was hard to concentrate because Payne kept grinding his hips up against me. "You were right honey. We should have video-taped it."

Jim laughed, "Ah sugar, there's no way I would forget you. Nice try."

I laughed and rolled Payne to his back. I was straddling him when I leaned down and kissed him. "Breakfast is ready. I have bagels, donuts, Pedialyte and aspirin for you. I need a shower."

"What's Pedialyte?" Payne asked.

"It's the stuff they give kids when they're dehydrated. Tommy swears it is the best thing for a hangover."

I got out of bed and walked up the stairs. I heard Jim say to Payne, "You lucky bastard."

I laughed as I headed up to my bedroom and began my morning shower. As much as my family was very casual, I wanted to look really good. I chose a long black skirt and evergreen colored turtleneck sweater. When I came downstairs to the kitchen, my mom was in the kitchen with Payne and Jim. They were sitting at the table with cups of coffee in front of them looking very much half dead.

I laughed. They winced at the noise.

"It's not funny. Your friend Sean is a lunatic." Payne commented as he sipped his coffee.

"Mom, Seanie told the entire bar that Jim was headed off to war and then bought all his drinks."

Chelsea's mom laughed. "It's a wonder you boys are still alive. You look nice Chelsea."

"Thanks. What time are Tommy and Julie coming over?"

"They'll probably get here around noon. Will you make sure the boys have what they need to get ready?"

"No problem. You boys ready?" I asked as they slowly got up from the table. Jim was still wearing his jeans from last night. "Jimbo did you even change last night?"

"I got the boots off and fell into bed." Jim answered with a smile.

I led them back downstairs and made sure there were towels for them. Jim hopped in the shower first. I made up the sofa bed and Payne sank down to the couch. I sat down on his lap.

"So how's the little man inside the head?" I asked.

"Working with a jackhammer." He answered.

I laughed.

"Just you wait." He said. "When we head out to Mc Sorley's tomorrow night. You won't be laughing so hard. You won't have to drive home and worm out of drinking with us."

He closed his eyes and leaned back on the couch. The basement door opened and I jumped off his lap like he was on fire. His eyes opened at the voice.

"Chelsea." My brother Tommy called, "Mom needs you."

"Coming." I called. "Remember I get my hands on him first." I leaned down and kissed him.

"Fine." He said tight-lipped.

I went upstairs to find Tommy, Julie and the kids there. The kids had already taken over the television.

"Chelsea can you run out to the garage and get the extra chairs. Tommy help your sister."

I walked out to the garage Tommy on my heels. I waited until we were inside the garage before I turned to him and punched him in the stomach.

"What the hell was that for?" Tommy asked.

"What the fuck were you thinking telling Steve where I was staying in Boston?" I was shaking with anger.

"You didn't tell me not to." He said rubbing his stomach.

"Tommy we need to talk about Steve." I said as he went hunting for the extra chairs. "And you better sit down in one of those chairs."

He took out a chair and sat with a sigh. "What's with all the drama Chelsea? Really so I told him where you were staying. No big deal."

"Why did you tell him?"

"I don't know. I guess I wanted to see what would happen if you had to choose."

"I made my choice when I didn't move to Boston with Steve. It had nothing to do with Payne and everything to do with Steve. As for it not being a big deal, it was a big deal. He showed up with a dozen roses to find Payne and I checking in. Payne told him to give up quietly. He didn't."

Tommy whistled. "I thought Steve was smarter than that."

"Not really. He showed up at the Barnes and Noble I was signing at. He and Payne had a discussion while I was signing."

"I would have paid to see that." Tommy said with a laugh.

"Not the kind of discussion you mean. Tommy," I paused. "Steve knew things that Payne didn't know. Things you don't know. Things Mom and Dad don't know. Things only I should have told Payne."

I took a deep breath. Tommy was looking at me intently. "You told him about the overdose. What else was there to tell?"

"Tommy, there wasn't one overdose. I tried the weekend before to drink myself into oblivion. It didn't work. I puked my brains out and passed out instead."

Tommy frowned. "Have you told Payne that?"

"Yes. But more importantly I told him the truth about the overdose. I told him why I did it." I paused again and Tommy looked puzzled.

"Tommy I was six weeks pregnant. I miscarried the night I overdosed."

Tommy dropped his head into his hands. I felt a huge rush of relief. I had finally told him. No more secrets.

"I'll kill him." Tommy said. "I'll kill him."

"He never knew. I never told him and you won't kill him. He wants to talk to you sometime today. I made him promise to let me talk to you first."

"You need to tell mom and dad." He said.

"No." I said adamantly

"Why not?" he asked.

"They had a hard enough time with it. I don't want to open it up all over again. Payne wants to make this work and I want to give him a fighting chance. I owe him that much."

"You don't owe him squat." He said getting up from the chair. He folded it up and headed for the door with two folding chairs in each hand.

"How would you feel if Julie had lost your child and never told you?"

He stopped at the door.

"I hurt him Tommy. I could have told him eight years ago. I could have told him anytime in the last six weeks. Instead a jealous irate ex-boyfriend told him his girlfriend was pregnant and rather than tell him, rather than have his child, she tried to kill herself not once but twice. YOU took that away from me by telling Steve where to find us last weekend. Now I'm taking this away from you. You will keep your mouth shut about the baby and you WILL be pleasant to Payne."

He nodded.

I picked up the other two chairs and went out the door in front of him. I loved having control over my older brother. It was a rare occasion. I had a smile on my face. When we walked back in the kitchen door, Jim and Payne were in the kitchen helping my mother. She had Jim getting hard to reach things on the top shelf and Payne was carrying things into the dinning room.

"What took you so long?" My mother asked.

"Tommy and I were having a little chit chat." I explained. Payne looked over at Tommy. Tommy nodded at him and brought the extra chairs into the dining room. My niece and nephew were in the living room with my father and Julie. I kissed Julie hello and began tickling my niece Alice. We were rolling around on the floor when Payne came in with Tommy.

"OK you guys leave Aunt Chelsea alone. If you want to watch your cartoons head downstairs to the basement. It's almost game time."

Payne, my father, Jim, and Tommy began watching the traditional Thanksgiving Day football games. They were absorbed in sports, and I had my little talk with Tommy. I could finally relax. I went into the kitchen to help my mother.

"Hey mom. What else needs to be done?"

"I'm shooting for half-time for dinner. Can you help me with the turnips and the mashed potatoes?"

"Sure." I answered. I began draining the boiled turnips preparing to mash them.

"How are things going with Payne?" My mother asked me.

"Really well." I said. "It's scary how well things are going. He's so different now. When he was in Philly he called me every Wednesday. He's tried to make up for lost time."

"Did you tell him about...."

"The overdose?" I said and she nodded. "Yes. He knows. We've been through a lot both together and alone."

"Are you happy?" She asked.

"Yeah mom. I am. For the first time in a long time, I'm really happy." I smiled.

"I'm happy for you. I spoke to your father about giving him a chance. If he knows you're happy, he'll be better with him. Are you finished?"

I nodded and put the turnips in the oven to stay warm.

"Go and show him how happy you are. It's easy to see when you are with him."

"Thanks mom."

I went into the living room and sat on the couch next to Payne. "Who's winning?" I asked.

He leaned over and kissed me, "Dallas."

"Not good." I said. He picked up my hand and held it in his. As we watched the second quarter, he rubbed his fingers across the palm of my hand. I would turn every once in a while to see him staring at me instead of the game. Halftime finally came. I went into the kitchen to help my mom start putting things on the table.

As I walked into the kitchen, I heard my father say, "Payne, can you help me get some more beer from the refrigerator in the garage."

CHAPTER 27

❀

I followed Chelsea's father out the side door to the garage. I was wondering what was coming. We were in the garage before he said anything to me. He had opened the refrigerator and began taking out beer.

"I really only have one question to ask you Payne and then we can head back inside." He handed me a six-pack of Carlsberg. "What are you planning to do about my daughter?"

"Sir …" I began.

"Hold on a minute and let me tell you where I'm coming from. I have a twenty-eight year-old daughter that should be married right now. She should have her own family. She doesn't. She asked me not to judge you by her actions. But that's a little hard to do. Last time she was involved with you I ended up getting a phone call in the middle of the night telling me my daughter had been brought to the hospital as the result of a suicide attempt. Someday when you have children of your own. You'll understand what a phone call like that does to you. I promised her I would let you prove yourself again."

"Thank you sir." I said. "I apologize for my behavior in college. I wish I had done things differently but I didn't. I've learned from my mistakes though. I love your daughter and I know she loves me. I wanted to speak to you this weekend about my intentions." I paused. My mouth was dry. "I would like your blessing to marry

Chelsea. I haven't asked her yet. I'm waiting until she's ready. She makes me happy and I want to make her happy. She's still learning to trust me, and I'm not going anywhere this time."

Her dad took all this in. He closed the refrigerator door and turned to me. "If Chelsea will have you, I have no problem with you two getting married. I trust her judgment." He held out his hand to me and I shook it. "You may have a harder time convincing Tommy."

"Tommy owes me right now." I said to her father as we walked back into the house. Her dad laughed.

"Tommy doesn't often dig himself a hole. I'd love to see him get out of it."

Chelsea looked nervous when we walked back into the house. I smiled at her and brought the beer into the dining room. She came up behind me.

"Is everything OK?" She asked.

"Everything is fine." I said. I turned to see her pale face. "Really Chelsea. Everything is fine. Your dad and I are fine. He said he trusts your judgment." I leaned down and kissed her.

We all sat down at the table. Tommy and Julie were across from Payne, Jim and I with a child on each side. Chelsea's father and mother sat at the ends of the table.

"Who's saying grace?" my mother asked.

"Grace!" The kids yelled and we all laughed at the usual joke.

"I'll do it." Tommy said. We were all a little shocked.

"Thank you Lord for the good food and the good company we have today. Keep Jim safe when he heads overseas in the next month. Thank you for returning Payne to Chelsea and making her happy again. Amen."

I was staring at Tommy. He was looking at Chelsea. She brushed away the tears from her eyes and turned to smile at me.

"Hey Payne." Her father said, "That was a pretty big hole."

I laughed and began passing the potatoes around the table. I decided to let the run-in with Steve go. Dinner and desert went amazingly smooth. Chelsea wanted to head back to her house on Thanksgiving night. Jim and I packed our things up and said good-bye to her parents. Tommy volunteered to drive us to the train station.

We all piled in Tommy's minivan and headed to the train station. At the train station, Jim and Chelsea got out of the back first and I hesitated in the car with Tommy.

"Tommy," I began.

"Listen Payne." He interrupted, "Chelsea pretty much put me in my place earlier. I'm sorry I told Steve where you guys were last weekend. I had no idea he would be such a prick and tell you about the baby. I didn't know."

"I wish I could tell you I'm all right with what happened. I'm not. She needed to tell me that, not Steve. You took that away from her. I want you to know, I plan on marrying her. She still needs some time, but I plan on being ready. I want to make her happy. She deserves it."

"From what I've seen you're off to a great start. I wish you nothing but the best." He put out his hand for me to shake it. I took it and for the first time saw a positive future with Tommy.

Tommy walked us to the platform and Chelsea hugged him goodbye. We were on the train before anyone spoke.

"So what is the plan of action tomorrow?" Jim asked.

"I have to work at the office tomorrow. I'll let Chelsea entertain you while I'm at work. Do you want to meet at my apartment?" I asked.

"Sounds good to me." Chelsea responded. She turned to Jim. "What do you want to do in New York?"

"I want to see Ground Zero." Jim answered. "After that I don't much care what I see. I want to see what I'm fighting for."

"OK." Chelsea answered. "From there we'll go over to Payne's apartment. Do you want to walk across the Brooklyn Bridge? That's really cool if it's a nice day."

We walked into Chelsea's driveway at around eight that night. Jim really hadn't seen her house when he arrived on Wednesday evening. Chelsea gave him the tour while I hung out in the living room. I was flipping around the channels when they returned to the living room.

"Do you want to stay here tonight?" She asked.

Jim looked like he was getting comfortable on the couch. He had kicked off his shoes and was stretched out.

"Jimbo, what do you want to do." I asked.

"I'm fine here on the couch. Where I'm going, the beds suck anyway. I might as well get used to it. I thought you said you loved her parents' sofa bed. That thing has the worst mattress."

"I didn't say I loved sleeping in it. I have fond memories of it is all."

"Gotcha."

"Listen." Chelsea began "I'm calling Susan's cell. She may be staying at Joe's tonight. If so you can take her bed."

She got up to call Susan from the kitchen.

"Did you talk to her dad?" Jim asked.

"Yeah." I said. "He said he trusts her judgment and I'm guessing I have Tommy's approval from his speech at grace."

"Do you have the ring yet?"

"I'm picking it up tomorrow. I only have to work a half day tomorrow. I'm heading to the diamond district to get it."

"A carat?"

"And a half." I said.

"Half of what?" Chelsea asked.

"Nothing," I said looking at Jim. "What's up with Susan?"

"Good news Jim. She's staying at Joe's place so you can have her bed."

"Unless you want me to sleep in your bed." Jim said wiggling his eyebrows.

"Nice try Jim." I said, "Chelsea, it's so obvious Jim is infatuated with you. We need to get him laid. Otherwise I may not wait for some road side bomb to get him, and I'll kill him myself."

Chelsea laughed. "I'm not about to volunteer for that cause. I don't know anyone who's still single."

Jim stood up and stretched. "I think I can take care of that all by myself. By the way, do not pull another stunt like last night. I'm no better than any other guy who's gone to war before me. I'd rather not be reminded that I'm doing a bullshit mission. Low key tomorrow night. OK?"

We both nodded and all three of us went up to bed. Jim went into Susan's room while Chelsea and I walked into her room. She undressed and put on a silk nightshirt. I hopped in bed in my boxers.

"What time are you due into work tomorrow?" she asked.

"Nine. Set the alarm for seven and I'll take it from there." I said lying on my side. "You want to tell me what you said to your brother to make him thank God for brining you and I back together."

"First, I punched him in the stomach."

I sat up. "You did what?"

"I would have decked him but he's too tall. I yelled at him about Steve. And I told him about the baby."

"What did he say about that?" I asked.

"At first, he wanted to kill you, but I talked him out of it."

"How?"

"I put him in your shoes. I asked how he would feel if Julie did what I did. That hit home. Julie had two miscarriages after my niece was born. They've given up trying to have more than the two children they have. It was very difficult for him."

"What about your parents? Did you tell them?"

"No. Someday maybe, but not now. You don't need that right now. I need to make it up to you."

"No you don't. I'd say we're even."

"What did my father and you talk about?" she asked.

"He wanted to know my intentions."

"And you said?"

"I told him it was my goal to make you happy. That's when he told me he trusted your judgment. He also told me I would have a more difficult time with Tommy than him. But you made it easier."

"You do make me happy." She said kissing me. "I can't remember being this happy. Ever."

I pulled her close to me and held her as she fell asleep. Somewhere in our crazy relationship just lying in bed with Chelsea in my arms became enough. I fell asleep thinking of the perfect way to ask her to marry me.

CHAPTER 28

The alarm went off at seven the next morning and I nudged Payne awake. He groggily got up and took his shower. I stayed in bed thinking about where to take Jim on his tour of New York City. I thought of working my way downtown with him until we reached Payne's apartment.

"Chelsea," Payne called from the door.

"Yeah." I answered.

"I'll call you when I'm done for the day. I may end early and we can hit McSorley's for happy hour. Keep your phone on."

"Goodbye kiss?" I called.

He came over and leaned over me. He kissed me quickly. "Gotta go. It's really bad if the supervisor is late. Love you."

He turned and walked out the door. I got up and tapped softly on the door to Susan's room. "Jim? Are you awake?"

"Yeah."

"Do you want to get a work out in?"

"Yeah." I turned back to my room and threw on workout clothes. I loved to take spinning classes and weight lifting classes. My gym offered both of them. I knew Jim had to be into working out since he was both an agent and an Army officer.

When we were both ready to go, I took him to my local gym and we went on our separate workouts. After we were done and walking home, I went through the plan for the day. The plan was to start out in Manhattan and work our way south to meet up with Payne either at his apartment or McSorley's. He wanted to see Times Square over Rockefeller Center and then head downtown to Ground Zero. Ground Zero was a solemn visit. We stood watching the work being done where the Twin Towers once stood. We were very quiet as we walked away. I was lost in the thought that Tommy could have been one of the over three hundred firefighters that had died that day. Jim confessed he was focused on the men and women lost in the battles after that day. I imagine he wondered if he would become one of the losses associated with that day.

As we were walking away from Ground Zero, my phone rang. It was Payne.

"Hey babe." I said. "Where are you?"

"I'm leaving work now. Where are you?"

"We just left Ground Zero. Do you want us to come back there or do you want to meet us at McSorley's?"

"McSorley's sounds good. Grab a table. Give me the address again?"

"East Sixth Street. Call me when you get close. Do you have the subway map I bought you?"

"Yes mom."

"If I was your mother we would have a serious problem. See you soon."

"Love you."

I hung up the phone. "He's meeting us at McSorley's."

"Can I make an observation?" Jim asked.

"Sure."

"You are so in love with him. When your phone rang and you saw it was him, your face lit up. He is so in love with you. He would walk through the fires of hell for you. And for what I gather the last six weeks have been hell for you two."

"Your point?"

"Why don't you tell him you love him? He says it to you all the time. In front of family and friends and I've never heard you say it back to him."

I was silent. I shrugged. "I don't know. I can't explain it. My life was pretty dark eight years ago and I built up some pretty tough defenses. He's gotten through most of them. I'm trying to let go but it's hard."

"Let go Chelsea. Leave it behind you. You need to bury the past and move forward. He's not going to leave you this time."

We had arrived at McSorley's. We walked in to find a pretty big crowd. As soon as a spot at a table opened up we sat down. About five minutes after we sat down, Payne arrived. He made his way back to us and joined our half full table. The waiter came over and we ordered six light beers and three hamburgers.

"What's up with the beer?" Jim asked.

"You have two choices for beer. Light or Dark. Light is like Sam Adams and dark is like a stout. You order in twos because the beer usually has too much head and spills as the waiter puts it on the table. He'll come over and want the empties later. They only offer hamburgers or cheeseburgers. One friend of mine tried to order a Coors light and wanted to see a menu. She almost had us tossed out."

We were laughing when the waiter came to the table and made my predictions true. We were on the third or fourth round when I noticed two women walk into the back room. I recognized one of them.

"Payne, isn't that Jen, my roommate from freshman year?"

"Popsicle Jen?" He asked. I kicked him under the table. Jen had spotted me and was coming over.

"Chelsea! Oh my god what's new?" She said hugging me. Jen was a bubbly blonde and with her was a very exotic looking petite brunette.

"Sit down with us." I said. "Do you remember Payne?"

"Oh my god. Yes! How are you?" Jen said.

"Great! I live in New York now. I'm with the ATF. This is my friend Jim Collins." Jim shook hands with Jen.

"This is my friend from high school, Nasrine."

"Hi." She said.

"Do you still live in Astoria?" Jen asked me.

"Yeah. I bought my grandfather's house. Are you still up by Newburgh?"

"Yeah. John and I got married four years ago and we have a little boy. What about you? Did you guys get married? I thought you broke up."

Payne answered her, "We did break up, but we're back together now. We're not married. Yet."

"Jim, do you live in the city too?" Jen asked.

"No. I live in Philly."

"No kidding. Nesrine lives down that way."

Jim turned to Nesrine. "Where?"

"Just over the border in New Jersey." She had long dark brown hair and was no more than five feet four inches with dark brown eyes. I could tell Jim was immediately interested. We invited them to join us at our table.

"Where are you guys going tonight?" I asked Jen and Nasrine.

"We were thinking of heading to Webster Hall and get a little dancing in." Jen volunteered.

"Sounds good to me. Jim, it's your vacation what do you think?"

"Dancing with these lovely ladies sounds like the perfect night." His southern accent became more pronounced.

"Nasrine. That's a cool name. What does is mean?" I asked.

"It means wild rose in Persian."

"Really? How did you get that?" I asked.

"My mother was from Lebanon. My last name is Smith. When you have the most common last name in the phone book, you tend to pick unusual first names."

"Her dad teaches at West Point." Jen volunteered. I thought I noticed Nasrine kick Jen under the table.

"Really?" Jim asked. "Are you in town visiting him?"

"Something like that." She said.

"You and Jen wet to high school together?" I asked.

Nasrine nodded.

"Catholic School?" Jim asked. When she nodded Jim continued, "Did you wear a uniform?" Jim nudged Payne when he asked that.

"Yeah." Nasrine answered. She looked puzzled by the question. I was puzzled more by their laughter. I knew there was something to this. I would have to get it out of Payne later.

We walked over to Webster Hall and went into to the dance club. I noticed Jim looking at Nasrine more than once. I was hopeful for Jim. She seemed like a nice girl. While I had known Jim a little more than a month, he deserved someone who cared about him. When we arrived at Webster Hall, Nasrine excused herself to the bathroom while I pulled Jim onto the dance floor. Payne was ordering drinks at the bar for all of us. I came back over to the bar as I heard Payne tell Nasrine about Jim and his deployment.

"Don't let Jim know that I told you, but he's being deployed in three weeks to Iraq."

"Really?" She said surprised. "So is this his going away party."

"Kind of. He's really low key. We took him out on Wednesday night and the bar made a big deal out of it." I explained. "My friend was the bartender and almost killed him with kindness."

As the night progressed, Jim became more interested in Nasrine and I thought she became more interested in him. I mentioned that to Payne. Payne's phone rang at one point. He got off the phone and dropped a bomb.

"I've got to go in tomorrow morning. Just for a little bit." he said checking his watch. It was almost midnight.

"Do you want to get going?" I asked.

"Yeah. Let me give Jim my apartment keys and my subway map. I'll stay at your place tonight. Things are looking good for Jim right now."

Payne went over and explained to Jim the situation. I saw him hand the keys and map to Jim. Jim came over and kissed me goodbye. We left Jim, Jen and Nesrine at the club.

We finally got home around one in the morning. Payne and I snuggled in bed. Payne got up at seven and kissed me goodbye.

"Love you." He said.

I rolled over and went back to sleep. Just before nine, I woke up and showered. I went downstairs and turned on the television. I was in the kitchen when I heard the news story.

"Two ATF agents were wounded in a raid this morning. One of the agents was a supervising agent. They were taken to Columbia Presbyterian. Their conditions are unknown at this time."

I dropped my coffee mug and ran to the phone. I dialed Payne's cell phone number. His voicemail picked up. I dialed his home phone. The answering machine picked up.

"Jim!" I yelled. "Jim. It's me Chelsea. Pick up!"

He picked up the phone. "Yeah." He said.

"Jim two ATF agents were wounded this morning. Did Payne tell you what he was doing today at work?"

"No. Chelsea calm down. Where did they take the agents?"

"Columbia Presbyterian. It's on one hundred sixteenth street in Harlem. Can you get me in?"

"Yeah." He said. I heard a muffled, "Can you get me to Columbia Presbyterian?"

"Sure." I heard in the background.

"I'll meet you there." Jim said to me.

I took the N Train and ran the two blocks to pick up the One Train to Columbia Presbyterian. My mind was racing with the grim possibilities. There was so much I hadn't said to him. I needed to see him. I needed to know he was OK. Jim was waiting with Nasrine outside the Emergency Room.

He showed his badge to security and dragged me with him. Nasrine followed. He requested information at the desk on the agents. They confirmed Payne had been wounded. I was beginning to panic.

"What is his condition? Where is he?" Jim asked.

"Are you next of kin? That information is only for next of kin." The receptionist said.

"Where is he?' I screamed.

"I'm right here." Payne said from behind me.

I turned to see him with his arm in a sling. I ran to him and threw my arms around him. He flinched.

"Easy." He said. "Stitches where the bullet grazed my arm and what I'm sure will be a very bad bruise come morning."

I was crying hysterically. I reached up and kissed him careful of his arm.

"Shh." He said, "I'm okay. Really."

"I couldn't think. I called Jim. I knew they wouldn't let me in to see you. I had to see you. I couldn't lose you again. I love you." I said.

He smiled down at me, "What did you say?"

"I love you. I was so afraid I wouldn't get a chance to tell you. I love you."

He dropped to his knee in the middle of the ER waiting room.

"What are you doing?" I asked. "Are you OK?"

"Chelsea Elizabeth Michaels will you marry me?" He reached into his pocket and pulled out a beautiful one and a half carat ring."

I was awestruck. "Oh my god! Yes! Yes!" I sank down to the floor and hugged him.

He slipped the ring on my finger and kissed me. I helped him up to his feet. The ER waiting room broke out in applause.

"Nice job buddy." Jim said. "Did you plan that one?"

"Nope. What were the odds I'd leave the ring in my coat at work?"

"Better than the odds of you getting shot on the raid."

"Will you two stop?" I said. "What is it with you and odds?"

"I don't know. I just love beating the odds."

I smiled and kissed him again. "You sure do. Let's get you home before anything else happens to tempt the odds."

978-0-595-46069-4
0-595-46069-0

LaVergne, TN USA
24 August 2009
155723LV00004B/7/A

9 780595 460694